# Stories from Tehran

## Expanded edition

ASEMANA
BOOKS

# Stories from Tehran

Expanded edition

# Fereshteh Molavi

ASEMANA
BOOKS

Toronto, Canada
FIRST EDITION

Published by ASEMANA BOOKS

Collection of short stories (originally written in Persian; translated into English by the author)

ISBN: 978-1-997503-08-8

Book Design: Asemana Books

Cover Art: Asemana Books

To find out more about our authors and books visit: www.asemanabooks.ca

ASEMANA
BOOKS

## *AUTHOR'S NOTE*

The stories were written in Persian in Tehran between 1980 and 1998. All the translations are my own. They are edited by Fraser Sutherland to whom I am grateful.

Fereshteh Molavi
Toronto, 2017

# Contents

# THAT SONG

The woman washes the dishes. It is a habit. It's a must. One should wash the dishes, that's all. But her shoulders are stiff. The water is warm and soft and greasy. She doesn't wear rubber gloves. Before turning on the hot water tap, she always looks first at her hands in pity; then she slowly puts on the rubber gloves. But in the middle of the task she grows sick of it. Her gloved hands sweat, the gloves tight and sticky. She gives up having beautiful hands. She takes off the rubber gloves and throws them away. Now her hands are soft and warm and greasy. It's disgusting. She grabs sodden lumps of bread and hauls them out of the water. When she puts in the inferior imitation Rika dishwashing liquid it doesn't produce enough suds; it doesn't get rid of the grease. But it does hurt the thin skin between her fingers. The greasy warm soft water in the pot isn't foamy white, but turbid and discoloured. When she uses the imitation Scotch-Brite dishcloth it shreds and gradually dissolves in the grease of the dirty water. The hungry stomach should be filled, so the dishes should be washed. The dirty hands should be ... no, she shouldn't dirty her hands. But only dirty hands can clean up stains. The dishcloth isn't working well. She scrapes with her nails. She shouldn't have put off washing so long that the leftover food and grease hardened and stuck to the plates and bowls and spoons and forks. The pile of dirty dishes offends her eyes. The glasses are better. The pots and pans are the worst. Her fine fingers, the soft tender skin, and those hands, those clean hands! What is far recedes further and what is nearby can't be seen. Why does something sting her back? That song ... that song ...

The wind blew. The cool breeze of October touched her skin and she pressed the warmth of the fresh *Sangak* bread against her hungry belly. In late afternoon the lane was quiet, the sky cloudy. The clamorous party of sparrows was breaking up. The tiny multi-coloured birds were tumbling leaves among wet branches. Like leaves, the grey sparrows sat on the ground and flew into the air. So where the hell did the afternoon sunshine atop those high bricked walls fly to? From the clothesline on the terrace the damp white shirt had stirred in the wind. But that song ...

One should stretch one's shoulders. One should wash the dishes. That's all. But her shoulders feel stiff and something stings her back and bites her skin. She pulls her hands back. She flexes her waist and straightens her back. She'd washed the shirt by hand and rinsed and shook it out. Maybe the wind had brought something like a thorn or a mote of dirt. Now the shirt, no longer white or damp, scratches her back between her shoulder blades, the spot where its heaviness presses on her. Without free hands, what can she do other than twist her body. The stiffness shifts from shoulders to spine and stays in her thighs. She shifts from one foot to the other. She raises her arm and wipes off the warm dampness on her temples. She turns her head and neck and wrinkles her eyebrows. The pile of dishes doesn't grow any less. She bends and pulls her shoulders forward. She takes her greasy and slippery hands out of the dirty water. She takes off the shirt and crumples it and rubs the skin between her shoulder blades with it. But the sting has lodged in the skin, and the bite isn't temporary anymore and there is no end to unwashed dishes and that song incessantly recedes.

... Or if it wasn't the wind that had brought the sting and it wasn't the damp white shirt stirring in the wind, then the sting has come from where that song has suddenly gone. As if there were no line between sleep and wakefulness. Her dirty hands wash the dishes, and her eyes see black, and the skin starts to smart and a sting that's no longer temporary at all lodges in the flesh too. That song incessantly recedes.

She closes her eyes. She could wash the dishes with her eyes closed and even in her sleep. She must wash the dishes with closed eyes and in her sleep. That's all. The nightmare and wakefulness mix. She can still clearly hear the howling dogs. They came at midnight and gathered beyond the window and barked. They still do that. She washed the dishes in her sleep and regretted not hearing that forgotten song. The dogs came every night and barked beyond the window. Every night the dishes mounted higher than the night before and that song went away further and the dogs barked louder than before. Such is still the case. Nonetheless the thin shivering line of the leaf's sound carried away by the wind ran between the dogs' barking. She still hears this thin line of sound.

So, it is the wind that carries away the leaf and that song along with the barking of dogs, and the thorn and the mote of dirt remains on the damp white body of the shirt. But the sting that has lodged in her back has passed through skin and flesh and reached the bone. As if there is no line in between sleep and wakefulness and one should wash the dishes. That's all.

# THE MIDNIGHT DRUM

He's just gone; he'll be back shortly. He said he'd be back soon, very soon. Maybe in an hour, or if he forgets his word, his promise, his commitment, he'll be back by 10 p.m. at the latest. She's done the dishes. She's putting her daughter to bed. Once again, she's left her sewing incomplete. Again, she's closed her half-read book. She's opened the skein of restlessness for another night.

Maybe she'd better go to bed. For the last time she calls on her kid and covers her body with the sheet. She winds up the alarm clock. She plugs in the electrical mosquito killer. She turns off the lights. Before going to bed as slowly and exhaustedly as always, she pauses to carefully review her evening tasks one by one. She's done everything -- all the small trivial domestic duties. Yet one obsessive habit still remains undone: she goes by the window and stands there; half bent, her elbows leaning on its dusty narrow edge, her palms underneath her chin. Is the ceiling of the sky high and far, or low and close? Is the moon visible or hidden? Is it cloudy or starry?

Tonight, it's a full moon; it appears and disappears. It slowly creeps behind hasty pieces of clouds and softly slips over them; it moves with October's cold breeze and breaks over the dark water of the pool in the yard.

Her knees bend. She restlessly lies on the bed. She pulls the blanket over her head and closes her eyes. Tonight, free from obedience, she should feel relaxed. No wonder that when he's home she's disturbed; that's why she hangs around in the kitchen until he goes to sleep; or she pretends she's sick; or she sleeps with him without passion or desire; or she just answers her own body's need without enjoying it. No wonder such a night, infected by hypocrisy, or horror, or surrender, is full of tension. Yet tonight, when she's alone, she shouldn't be restless. She could feel calm and comfortable now if tonight were not polluted with this poisonous anticipation. The day hides panic and unrest with its dazzling light, with ceaseless movement, with the load of duties and errands. Whereas the night tears apart the hypocritical cover of the day with its darkness and acquiescence and leaves her alone and vulnerable in a crippling draft. Why doesn't she go to a sleep free from a dream or a nightmare? Why is she so obsessed to avoid a mere surrender? Why can't she lend herself to a bold rebellion? She can neither stay nor escape.

A car engine's sound falls upon the soundless moan of her worries. She pulls away the blanket involuntarily and sits on the bed, motionless. She listens alertly. What should she do if it's him? Should she remain sitting there to blame him with her silence? Or should she vent her anger by nagging? Or maybe she should pretend she's asleep? The sound grows nearer, then recedes, and finally dies away as it passes the lane and leaves her alone in her fervent silence.

She doesn't want to sleep anymore. Sitting on the edge of bed, she gazes through the window. A piece of sky, half cloudy, half moonlit, framed in an ugly metal windowpane, a flowerbed sunk in a disturbed illusion, and a small shallow pool — all are her share from the whole external night. This share she can admit humbly is fair enough. But within her internal night she gets more than her share.

She should get up; maybe she can shake this rust off her body and soul. She stands by the window again. She stares again at the moon half-lit, half visible — the same moon at which she stared while she waited for him; the moon whose beauty and grace reduced the bitterness of waiting. But no, this moon is not the same moon. She's no longer young to flatter herself with a delusional love. Neither is she old enough not to desire love. It is October, a cold October. Her home is quiet, a cold silence. No wonder her husband flees from this sly early cold, yet... no, he doesn't have the right. There is no right. None of them has a right, or love, or affection. Both are bound to a painful lying commitment. They are unequal though. The same punishment for different sins; or perhaps for a different innocence. They soothe the suffering differently. Her husband pretends he is almighty. He goes wherever he likes, he does and says whatever he wants. He is the boss of the house, he has the custody of their child, and he is the lord of his wife. She soothes herself deceitfully too, though in a different way. He deceives himself rather than her; he relieves the pain more than she does. Her inevitable solution is a very old-fashioned one, a womanly surrender -- that kind of surrender contaminated by hypocrisy, shrewdness, and cowardice. Though it hides her helplessness, this deceit makes her more wounded.

Once again, she feels weak at the knees. She lies on the bed again. She listens to her daughter's quiet breathing. She pushes her face against the pillow and presses her eyelids. She's falling asleep. She hears a sound.

The sound came closer. She didn't want to wake up. She turned over. Nobody was beside her. "He's gone for a walk," she thought. The sound was drumming on her thin sleep: they were sailing over the water. It was sunset. The sea was green – of varied greens, like the wheat field of those early years. *She was standing in the middle of the field. Up there, a bird was turning in the centre of the azure dome. It was hemming patches of clouds with the silky thread of its chirp.* Here, behind the horizon, the sun was sinking into the sea. The boatman was looking at the horizon. *There, in the middle of the field, she was lovingly looking at a man who was busy digging damp soft soil with a stick. Above, the bird was turning over and over.* Here, she bent over the edge of the boat and sank her hand into the water. She could feel the warmth of her husband's thigh, yet she was dreaming, asleep with the water. The sharp cry of a seagull ripped into her delicate dream. With envious eagerness her husband was staring at a young couple sitting at the other side of the boat, kissing and cuddling. She felt indignant. She wanted to prod him, but she changed her mind. She turned away. Again, she sank her hand into the soft and cool water. Again, she closed her eyes.

The sound was incessantly drumming with more vigour over the relaxed sleep of a woman who recovered without regret from the exhausting tension of an old love. Behind her closed eyes, the sound was coming up from the narrow steep stone-paved lanes of Istanbul to fall upon the sleep of her body tired of the journey.

She turns over. More and more she pushes her face against the pillow. She doesn't want to know what sound brutally overwhelms her daughter's quiet breathing. The sound was constantly drumming and ripping up the fine fabric of her dream. She had got up angrily and sat on the bed. Her husband had been standing by the window, smoking. He hadn't gone out. Annoyed by her cold unkindness, he had been leaning against the corner of the wall, looking at the lane through the lace curtain. She had asked about the sound. "It's the drum telling people to wake up. The midnight drum of Ramadan," he'd said bitterly, without looking at her.

They were wandering around the lanes proclaiming it. The shadows were approaching and proclaiming something. The drums were waking those who overslept. She was not sleepy anymore. She had awakened and discovered she was not in love anymore. The drums seemed to proclaim that she was free of her old love. They were publicly announcing that she didn't love her husband anymore; that at nights she dreamed of unknown men as she was sleeping beside her husband and that, during the day, terrified and embarrassed, she wore the mask of a chaste obedient spouse. It looked as if the drums were pulling away from her body and soul all the layers of deceit.

The drumbeats of bygone years, the proclamation of hidden shame, are still in her ears. When she's asleep, or home alone at night, the crazy rapid drumbeats make her feel dizzy. The shadows approach and the drums proclaim. She becomes disgraced and naked. She is waiting for footsteps, or the echo of the doorbell's ring. She's looking forward to hearing news. Poison in her throat, she's waiting — a black waiting contaminated by hatred and malicious desire for his death.

She's shocked by the horrible attack of a sound, the drumbeat's proclamation. She jumps up. The darkness, the loneliness, the body's shivering, and the familiar sounds — a motor engine, footsteps, a key turning in the lock. Another midnight has arrived already. Another night she is torn apart by the uproar of the drums. Another night the man returns to make her malicious waiting defeated by the fact of his presence.

# THE INDIAN CROW

By the song of a crow, by the dance of light on the shade of dreams, by the scent of a tropical morning, I woke up in Delhi. Awakening. Spring. The awakening of spring, and the pleasure of a trip. Parting the cotton curtain, I open the window. The quiet courtyard of the hotel, the smooth sunbathing willow, ash, and eucalyptus in the small garden, and the familiar fuss of sparrows subdue nostalgia and anxiety. I get up. I shower. I don't look in the mirror.

The gaze of the young man's big black eyes at the reception desk makes me feel light, like a "leaf in the wind..." The glass of warm milk slowly turns in my hands. I inhale milk's good smell. The light green of the lawn beyond the glass door touches my eyes with its wetness, softness. The young man says that today is the festival of Holi and if I go outside people will scatter colours on me. I smile at his face, his gaze, his words. I leave the hotel. I turn my eyes away from the colonial bow that the slim, thick-lipped, dark-skinned doorman makes.

The quiet street of a holiday. I walk. A pleasant warmth, my uncovered head, my hair falling loosely to my shoulders, a day of wandering, and a meeting to come that night. Someone calls me. I stop and turn my head. An Iranian family: parents with their two kids. They've come here for their spring vacation. The woman is disconcerted by this unexpected holiday, and happy to find a Persian-speaker like me. She is outgoing and chatty and would be good company — even if inquisitive. After asking a couple of questions, she realizes that I don't know whatever she wants to know. I have no idea about prices and how to get the best deals. Though she's a bit disappointed, the fact I know the streets, and the bazaar is good enough for her. It's good for me, too, to hear her nice voice and her sweet accent. Her words sail past my ears into the breeze. Just arrived, she's unhappy that they haven't gone to Thailand instead of coming here. It would have been cheaper there, and they could have found better things to buy. Just think, years have passed and there are still many problems about travelling abroad, especially in wartime, and only enough money to get to India. Although her husband is a customs officer and knows what to do, it's after all a strange country. Even though she's smart she'll still get cheated. The foreign currency they have with them isn't enough to visit everywhere and to buy souvenirs for relatives and friends. With them they've taken a little smuggled foreign currency, and a few things they can sell: choice pistachios, almonds, and saffron, and gold, gold, gold. Where can one sell these things? Dealing ... dealing ... dealing ... a greed for dealing ... the leprosy of dealing ...

For me, only a voice, simply the voice and melody of words, and with them lost or disconnected familiarities and associations. Words are nothing but wind. The soft warm wind ruffles my loose-fitting dress. Looking at the woman's hair, which is thick, oak-coloured, long, and loose, I smile. We both breathe freely here. She has a long-sleeved dress; she's thinking about buying some t-shirts, though. So many things she wants to buy: sari, sandals, a headscarf with golden threads, a night gown, earrings and necklaces, ivory bracelets, bedcovers, a Cashmere shawl, silk. Things and things ... colours and colours ... Watch out, someone might sprinkle colours on her!

A cyclist passes with smiling face and threatening hands. He leaves behind a trace of mingled colours. A bus passes. A bunch of young shabby guys with dark faces, white teeth, and stained hands poke their heads from windows and laughingly strew fistfuls of colours over us. I try to clean up my face with my hands, but apparently, I make it worse. Looking at their mother and me, the woman's two sons burst out laughing. We look around, but there's no water tap.

Beside a shady avenue is a narrow channel. I reluctantly wash my face in its muddy water. The kids tell me that my ears are still red and my forehead green. I don't like to return to the hotel now. An old yogi has squatted beside the channel. He is expressionless, empty as the bowl next to his hand. Once again, a gang of youths noisily approaches us with colours. This time I don't avoid them. I'm now immune. We laugh. We and the kids laugh and head toward the youths. Dark skin, glittering eyes, dry lips, big white teeth, worn-out rags, crusted bare feet, and coloured hands. The colours: green, red, yellow, purple, and blue. Cheap joys. I hear their heartbeats. The trembling warm weather.

The trembling waving warmth, the smell of sweaty bodies; people who pass and disappear; people who passed and disappeared. And another scene, this one in the past: a seventeen-year- old girl disappearing into the feverish fuss of a crowded bazaar. Above her a near, pure, blue, and empty sky. Around her were all noises, all colours, all things, all people. The sweet traces of *Zahedi* dates in her mouth, the mild smell of bananas in her nose. Fragrance of perfumes and fruits; the scent of Lux soap and of tea, the scent of Yardley face cream, the aroma of spices. The booths, tables, and shops. The shopkeepers, sellers of smuggled goods, and the buyers. Villagers, townsmen, and Kurds on horseback with rifles over their shoulders. Donkeys, automobiles, and bicycles. The noise, hubbub, colour, and smell. Ghasr-e Shirin, a city in Iran, and its palms; Ghasr-e Shirin and its heat-stricken lanes; Ghasr-e Shirin and the heat waves of its summer; Ghasr-e Shirin and its small low houses; Ghasr-e Shirin and her dreams when she was seventeen; Ghasr-e Shirin and her constant search, her unbounded passion, her gaze, her blushing cheeks, and the fast beating of her heart.

I hear the heartbeats of the seventeen-year-old girl of Ghasr-e Shirin in the warmth of Delhi. I hear her heartbeats, their heartbeats.

Wandering around the streets. Tourists with naked tanned thighs and arms, cameras slung around the neck or over shoulders, with sandals and wreaths of small yellow and orange and white flowers. Strutting flower-decked cows. Stern turbaned Sikhs. Women and silk, satin, and cotton saris, with black plaits, bare pulpy brown tummies, sockless feet, coloured lips, big eye-linered eyes, and cute *bindis*, the red or black dots on their foreheads. Dark-complexioned children with twiggy legs and open mouths. Defeated men slowly walking, men lying on soil and lawn and stone of parks and streets and lanes, men with big stomachs, thick lips, and greasy skins, skinny men of hunger and dashed hopes. Skyscrapers crowded next to low stone and brick buildings. Wide, quiet, and shady avenues on which travel small old automobiles, worn-out motor rickshaws, and crummy bikes. Old Delhi: the hurly-burly of a Bedouin invasion of motion and noise, the crazy mingling of the nastiness of poverty and the dynamism of life.

Nehru Park. The tranquility of a pleasant evening. I hear plants breathe. I look around, but I don't see him among the guests. I bet he'll come, though. Dark servants in white, some of their uniforms stained or grubby, are serving drinks and appetizers to guests of all colours. Clusters of people gather in corners. It's half an hour before the program of traditional dances. A middle-aged host approaches me with a small plate of colours and offers to put a spot on my forehead. I boringly tell him that I'd been adorned that morning. I avoid familiar faces. I linger restlessly. I find a free chair in a cozy corner. An umbrella of leaves over my head, a green carpet under my feet, the caress of moving air on my hot skin, a forgotten line on the lips of my silence: "Leaf in the wind ..." Memory disquiets my mind. "Leaf in the wind, I go at the drift of my dreams." Which poet wrote, which lips said, this poem? Which lover, which heart, hid regret in this way?

When I met him this week the Venetian had asked me how old I was. I said I was thirty-seven. He said he didn't believe it. When I smirked, he lowered his head. He pressed my arm gently. I softly, slowly repeated: thirty-seven. He shrugged and said that he wasn't young either. He was seven or eight years older, and this meant that sometimes he lost confidence. He asked me how old my daughter was. I said, "Seventeen and ... "He said, "And what? I said, "Seventeen and alone, and bombs are falling in Tehran." He interrupted and said that his stepdaughter was the same age. He said that she lived with his wife in Rome, far from him. He said he missed them very much. He said that and pressed my arm again.

A sky near the sunset hour. I'm alone. Restless heart. Confused mind. The wet green pressure of plants on the dry skin of my loneliness. A garden in Delhi. A small garden in Venice.

Azad Street in Delhi — and Azad means "free". A cow regally proceeds down the street, gentle and oblivious. The wreath of flowers around her neck swings softly. She looks peaceful. A man slowly walking behind her. April morning. Azad Street, an avenue full of leafy trees, their branches kinked and twisted. Sitting on a bench, I feel the warm wet wave of rainy tropical forests. I see the dense forests light, not dark. Sunshine, a world-illuminating sunshine, the mild sunshine of Delhi's early spring, the sunshine of Iran, my sunshine, my sunshine above my head. Light leaves. Light green leaves, light yellow and red and orange leaves. A gardener is cutting the fresh lawn of a government building. Wet green needles shower from under the blade. The clear murmur emerging from the larynx of fountains mingles with the breeze and slides across the air. The rustling of the street-sweeper's broom scratches the thin curtain of silence. A pile of burned leaves smokes and spirals in the clear air, the smoke disappears. Chattering of sparrows, song of small bright birds whose names I don't know, and ... the crows. Once in a while, a pedestrian or a cyclist passes leisurely. Far from the noise of metallic invasion, I sip the fresh clean morning with all my senses. Lightness, warmth, freshness permeates me. At thirty-seven, I feel young because of this desire for freshness. The warmth of a desire hidden under snow, the heavy snow of fled moments, of piled experiences, and of settled fatigue and frustration, suddenly revives me. The rebellious tree moves its body. I will go to his home, to the Venetian's home. I suppress my doubts about riding on a cycle rickshaw. The cyclist is young, dark, and bony. The tight muscles of his brown legs, the bulged veins of his neck, the running thread of sweat over the back of his neck, the constant movements of his slim body, and the snail's pace of his bike again make me ashamed that I have put him to this effort. I am disappointed at myself, as if I had swallowed the rickshaw, this medieval remnant, this piece of stale mouldy bread, without knowing how to digest it. I bite my lip. My disappointment and shame compensate for the fare — for him the cost of a sandwich and a movie ticket.

In my mind I try to avoid whatever may hide his face. I close my eyes to the long way, the uneven road, maddening noon heat, and lethargic hesitation in the middle of the way. I'm trying to find the Venetian's place in search of love, or passion, or happiness, or whatever it is that I've lost.

Now he opens the door. Startled, he stares at me. The heavy sad look of a lonely man shadows my passionate willingness. I'm happy, though, that I've come to his home to be with him. He says gently and slowly that he thought I'd left. I say I don't go today, but tomorrow ... He puts his hand on my lips and begs that we don't think about tomorrow. Closing my eyes, I say to myself that's what I want -- not to see tomorrow. But tomorrow has stuck in my mind, looming. I sit in the only armchair in the room. Noting with satisfaction his childlike happiness, I only half-listen to him. He talks non-stop. He is restless. He has innocently opened his heart to this unexpected joy. I regretfully tell myself how easily he believes in it. How naturally! He's still able to be as happy as a boy. So, he's not old. But I've just come here to believe that love has passed me by, that it never will return, that now by myself, like a leaf in the breeze, I move where my faded dreams blow. Nonetheless, on my last day here, I'm happy to be with this stranger, this nostalgic unknown Venetian. My joy is mingled with the sorrow of a lonely woman who knows she's lost love forever.

Curtain after curtain, darkness softly falls. "What else?" he asks. I say nothing. What can I say? The Venetian wants me to speak. He's not as childlike and cheerful as he was at noon. Just as he believed that I was about to leave, he again anticipates losing me. His anger exceeds his frustration, yet he disguises it with constant talk.

We go out. With him at my side, I'm not afraid of Delhi at midnight. I feel relaxed. He says he wishes I could forget everything tonight. I don't reply. He knows that I can't forget. The first time I met him, he asked about the war with Iraq, and reminded me of Ghasr-e Shirin. I recalled that Ghasr-e Shirin of twenty years go, the town of that passionate girl seeking love. But now the horrible shadow of a ruined Ghasr-e Shirin, the border town that was an Iraqi target, is between us, between him and me, with me not with him, the shadow stalks me. He says making love is nothing but expressing sympathy. Isn't that right? I shrug. I'm not looking for solace in the same way he is.

Curtain after curtain, darkness softly falls. The darkness hid that garden in Venice, the small garden of a Venetian inn. My daughter, seven years old, had fallen sleep in my feverish bosom. A full day of lingering in the narrow lanes of Venice, watching strangers, the strange spectacle, the odd sense of walking on water, and the welcome burden of my daughter's small soft body, could not repress the insistent desire for love.

I hold the Venetian's arm, saying that I wish I could have seen him when I'd been twenty-seven. He smiles and asks if it was when I visited Venice. I nod. "With your family?" he asks. I nod. He smilingly asks if it was there that I realized I didn't love my husband anymore. I don't respond. A sky full of stars over my head, a stranger beside me, and the weight of the nightmare of horrible loneliness weighing me down.

We reach a lighted street. We pass by a movie theatre. A bunch of beggars invade us. Most of them are kids. Another stale mouldy piece of bread that must be swallowed. The kids are clutching my hands and skirts from every direction. When one disappears, another one replaces him. Nothing's left in my purse. He reminds me again that if I start giving them money, I won't be able to stop. We quicken our pace. His calmness disturbs me. He says that's because I'm not used to beggars. A young girl holding a baby doesn't give up. She follows us for several metres. For a moment, I sense that she is chasing me with a ladle of the thin peppery broth that they drink. I want to run. He pulls my arm and tells me to relax. I tell myself that I can't. Finally, the girl gives up. Cursing us, she angrily kicks an empty tin can towards us. The Venetian bursts into laughter. He asks me if there aren't any beggars in Tehran. I don't respond. I hate myself. I say to myself that Tehran has beggars, and homeless war veterans, and on top of that the sky delivering ...

At the end of Delhi's night, I still walk with him, aware of his presence, yet shadows tighten their hold on me: Ghasr-e Shirin, Venice, Delhi; seventeen years old, twenty-seven years old, thirty-seven years old. I've detached myself from the April's morning of Azad Street. At the end of Delhi's night, I feel as if I still hear a croaking. The Indian crow, hidden in the dark, shreds my dreams.

## OFFENCE

Was the cover they draped over the guillotine in Andrzj Wajda's film *Danton* offensive or frightening? Did it conceal the offence, or horror, or savagery? Maybe it was only meant to protect the blade from rust. She didn't want to think about the scene when the cover was pulled off. Somehow, she was avoiding that. She was skipping that, imagining other scenes. What was the expression in Danton's or the others' eyes as they were trundled in carts through narrow lanes toward the place of execution? Was that expression of fear, or regret, or bewilderment that they'd been fooled? When the job was done and a woman tied a thin red thread around her neck, she became more confused. First, she thought that it was the end of the movie, but it went on.

  She got up. The house was empty and quiet. Her husband had gone to work. He had taken the kid to day care. Last evening she'd told him that she wouldn't go to work tomorrow. She had asked him to take the kid to day care because she had to go shopping. She opened the sewing box. There was no red spool. She closed the box. She dug into the basket of yarn. She didn't have any red yarn either. She bit off a piece of thick black yarn.

She stood in front of the mirror and, exactly like the woman in the film, she wound it around her neck. She didn't tie it. She stared at her reflection. Her mind became full, yet empty. It didn't reach a conclusion. She crumpled the yarn in her fist. She wore her *manteau* (Islamic uniform for women). She thrust the yarn into her pocket. She glanced at the clock. She had to hurry. She remembered that she had to eat something. It was Ramadan. She reluctantly drank the tepid cup of tea. She couldn't swallow a bit of stale bread. There was no butter or cheese. Just in case she got hungry, she put a piece of bread in her bag. She'd likely be able to find a cozy corner or quiet lane somewhere to eat it.

Having closed the door, she paused, thinking. She'd brought along all the ration and bonus coupons for the New Year. Today she didn't have to worry about punching the clock at work and the stealthy look of the person in charge of watching employees. She hadn't filled out the form for the leave. She didn't plan to ask for sick leave. It wasn't worth it. When her kid was sick or she had to do errands, she'd take it off her vacation time. The fridge and freezer were empty. In the middle of the lane, she remembered she hadn't taken plastic bags with her. Damn it! She would buy them. What mattered was to come back home with hands full of stuff.

Before reaching the bus stop, she had time to think and plan in order not to waste a day off. Homemakers, even if they had to leave a child alone at home, don't hurry their shopping. Going around lanes and finding the right queues are time-consuming jobs. Sometimes it might even be fun.

The morning sunshine, shiny white satin patches. She passed by the mosque, hearing the voice of the Koran reader. The April sunlight fled and vanished, then clouds filled their share of the sky. The sun's face disclosed itself again. A cold pale sun. A lane without the scent of spring, bare branches. She couldn't believe that spring would arrive before May. Where was May?

No longer were there any signs of the black-draped, mirror-ornamented *hejlehs*, representing the wedding chambers of unmarried young men, new martyrs in the war, with memorial candles and framed photographs strewn with flowers. She tried to avoid looking at the wall flyers announcing deaths, martyrdoms, or other bad news. She quickened her pace. At the corner of a lane, she noticed a queue. Likely the local co-op store had things at subsidized prices. Before reaching it, she decided to drop into the grocery store. She wanted to ask if her card for milk was still valid. Ali Aqa's grocery store was as dirty inside as it looked outside. Carefully putting a few eggs into a woman's plastic bowl, Ali Aqa was noisily scratching his unshaven chin.

"Three of them are cracked," said the woman.

"So what? I didn't break them," Ali Aqa laughed.

"But I'm not buying these eggs with ration coupons. I'm paying five *tomans* (currency of Iran) each."

"Madam, don't make me grumpy this early! There's no difference between the free market and coupons about this. The customer should take the cracked eggs."

The slim, olive-skinned woman wore a black cotton headscarf. Ali Aqa put the fifth egg in her bowl and said, "If you don't want it, you can go somewhere else..."

"But..." was all the woman said.

Ali Aqa wiped his dirty hand on a shirt that was as dirty as a dish cloth and impatiently turned to another customer.

When she reached the line-up, she asked, "Madam, what are they distributing?"

"Cheese if you've got coupons."

"This co-op store almost never brings stuff to sell on its own. We should be grateful it sells stuff for coupons, though."

"That's why it's not busy. It doesn't even ask to see members' coupon booklets.

"In the last six months all that any member got was two pairs of plastic gloves."

"What the hell do we need gloves for, when we can't afford to buy dish detergent?"

"We could go to the square and sell the gloves."

It was her turn. She gave her coupon to the man, but as soon as she saw the plastic bag of cheese, she changed her mind: "Aqa Shams, this looks like condensed yogurt."

"Better for you!"

"But it might look like this because it's too stale."

"The taste is the same, sister. You haven't got used to eat what's given to you and thank God.

"Madam, don't waste people's time. If you don't like foreign cheese, buy some from Tabriz, 400 tomans a kilo."

She smelled the cheese, growing suspicious. She was jostled from the back. She forced her way out. She saw the bus. She ran and, panting, dragged herself up the steps. It was packed. She stretched her hand and flung the ticket. The driver was testy:

"Why did you throw it at me?"

"I didn't, sir..."

"Yes, you did. You don't know who I am! You should give me the ticket politely. How long have you been living here?"

She blushed. The veins in the driver's neck bulged.

"You should be ashamed..." she said.

"What the hell are you saying? *You* should be ashamed because you think I'm your father's chauffeur..."

"Driver, say *salawat*, humble respects to the Prophet and his Family," somebody said as a way of making peace.

But she was angry. Thank God the bus was so packed she was enclosed in a wall of flesh.

She stepped down at the last stop. She got herself lost in the crowd at the edge of the square. She felt a stab of pain in her temples. She was sure she hadn't meant to be rude or insulting. Now that fresh air reached her face, she could tell herself that she'd made an unintentional mistake. Certainly, the driver had been in a bad mood. One of the passengers had joked, "Maybe this morning he was fighting with his wife about money." Anyway, the incident had pissed her off. She was glad that she'd said, "From dawn to midnight you're insulted but you don't protest..." That bully could have protested in the right place. But she didn't speak up either.

There was a morality-squad patrol parked in a corner of the square. A crowd was around it. She peeped in. A woman in a chador, part of her chin covered by a *maqna'eh* (full head cover), said:

"In Ramadan they should be ashamed to bother these sisters when they're fasting."

Another woman, ignoring the first, said, "If I knew that I'd be given a pair of black trousers as a reward, I'd have worn sheer nylons too."

A young guy, giggling, said, "They take them into the car and then let them go all cleansed."

She looked so confused that an old man, nodding, said:

"They clean up the women's make-up."

She left the crowd behind. Madam Andalibi, the superintendent of her high school when she was a teenager, had behaved like the morality squad. Short and chubby, with a deep voice and bolster-like legs, stumped forward when she approached you. She used to swing her ruler in the air and stand at the front door of the high school. First she examined girls' nails. Any hands with coloured nails got a blow from her ruler. Then it was time to examine the skirts. She thrust her plump fingers into the girls' waist to make sure they hadn't tucked in their skirts. If the skirts were short, she would rip out the stitches, no matter if the girls begged or cried. Having performed the anti-miniskirt operation, she stared at the faces of her prey with her small black inquisitorial eyes. To make sure they weren't wearing lipstick, she sometimes rubbed her thick thumb against their lips. Finally, she inspected the hair. If the girl's hair was puffed, she would thrust her fingers into it and drag the girl to the bathroom, pushing her head under the tap. Yet for some reason there were more girls who ignored this probable punishment than those who didn't take the risk. For there was always a chance to skip her eyes and hands when she was busy with prey, and during recess it was possible to avoid her eyes.

Now she instinctively pulled forward her maqna'eh. When she was in elementary school, she thought that no humiliation was worse than wearing a dunce cap and being forced to walk around the classrooms. When she entered high school, she realized that being caught by Madam Andalibi was much worse.

Now where should she go...? The ministry's special co-op store had frozen French chickens for those who had a members' booklet. The line-up was so long that people at the end of the queue started to worry that they wouldn't get chicken. The noon sun was strong. Her back hurt. Her mouth had dried. She hesitated over joining the line or giving up. It was always like that. First, she'd confidently join a line-up. Then gradually she got impatient. All that for a piece of meat... But this piece of meat could go on her son's plate... She should control herself. In order not to leave the line-up, she began to amuse herself by listening to people.

A man passing the queue, loudly said, "Look at them! Instead of sitting at their desk responding to the public, they're busy getting stuff morning till noon."

His words agitated the queue. Some laughed. Some grumbled. Some cursed. The men's queue became disorderly. Women jostled and complained.

"Madam Hoseini, watch your purse so your coupons won't get lost!"

"After all, all this is good for tea-ladies, janitors, and telephone operators. They buy and sell the stuff and..."

"But these guys just take little bites, what about the people who sit on the management board for a while and make a big haul?

"Eventually we never figure out what they did."

"Don't we? Now they're taking it easy and laughing at us."

"But if we didn't have this co-op, we'd have to open our mouths and let something drop into them out of the sky."

"It's been seven years since I've asked for a TV set. Not my turn yet, though."

"Nonsense! Thank God everything's available in this country. If you'd seen the famine during the World War..."

She remembers the film. The French Revolution, par excellence. People are crushing each other in a rush to get a slice of bread. They are frantic to see Danton. Danton, in his coach, hears their crazy adulation and laughs.

"Did you see any movies at the film festival?"

"I'm not that much of an idiot to line up to see movies."

"Don't you stay in line to buy *Zulbiya Bamiyeh* dessert?"

"Madam, go ahead! It's the women's turn."

The French chickens had melted. Two plastic bags weren't enough. Blood and water mingled at the bottom of the bag. Eventually she'd come out with hands full of stuff, but her arm hurt suddenly from the pressure of the crowd. She collected the change from the bottom of her purse. She bought another plastic bag from the booth next to the main entrance. The box of insecticide had got wet. She tried to firmly close it, she failed. Her hands stank of insecticide. She loudly swore.

The vendor, who still had his country village's felt hat on, said, "Madam, who are you talking to?"

"I'm talking to the toilet cockroaches," she answered angrily.

If she hadn't used up the coupon number in her members' booklet to get this damned Baygon insecticide, she would have thrown it in the water channel at the curb and...

On her way, she reached the Qods chain store. She saw a pack of sanitary napkins in a woman's hand. She stopped for a moment. She put her bags on the ground. Her shoulders were stiff and sore. But it would be a pity to miss the chance. She took a deep breath and entered the store. When she was in the line-up at the cash register, she saw a sanitary napkin in the hand of a boy waiting in the line. She looked at him, surprised. She decided to be rude. "Do boys need sanitary napkins?"

But the boy was ruder than she was. "None of your business"

She turned to the cashier and said, "But madam..."

The cashier raised her thin eyebrows. Tired, she said, "What can I do? These guys should make a living too. They do it everyday. After all, you could get a pack too..."

Now her load was so heavy that she was staggering. She had forgotten to gobble her stale piece of bread in some corner. Even if she could have remembered, she wouldn't have felt like it. She passed the Sepah chain store. Like yesterday and the day before, the horde of chadored women were making a fuss about getting cooking oil. In a moment the store would be closed. The crows of sunset were croaking. Drops of sweat ran from the back of her ears. The weight of her shopping load dragged at her shoulder blades: down -- maybe down to the ground, or even underground. She had put aside some leftovers last night for today's lunch. But, turning the key in her door, she'd certainly hear her husband, yelling like a demon, "Where the hell were you?"

The vacant lot at the lane's entrance went uphill. The distant mountain was visible. Panting, she dragged her feet, her load, and her tired body. She didn't look at the garbage around herself. She looked at the mountain in the distance. She saw the scene when the cover was taken off the guillotine. She shouldn't avert her eyes from that. She shouldn't look down. She didn't have the strength to carry the load anymore — the load that was dragging her hands and arms and shoulders down. Why had she avoided looking at the guillotine and its cover? Now the cover had been pulled off, the metal blade gleamed at the edge of the twilight. But now she was not afraid anymore. She had to free her hands from the heaviness of the load. She had to rest the load on the ground of the vacant lot so that she could go ahead. She thrust her free hand into her pocket and crumpled the black thread in her fist.

# THE OTHER WAY ROUND

## I

What wonderful weather, what a wonderful spring! I turn my face to the breeze. My feet move forward; my hands move free. The quiet lane between gardens and the mountain whose top is crisscrossed with the remaining snow; the soft delicate green of weeping willows; the spiral sun-dried brick wall of the Colonel's garden. I keep my distance — beyond the wall, blossoms of plum and cherry and peach. I walk slowly. Why should I stop? Further on, another garden; further yet, another mansion; further still, another tree. I breathe deeply. Why should I hurry? The path rises. I walk ahead carefully and slowly. I keep my eyes open. The stupid hands of the clock remain behind me. The smell of wet soil and tender grass. What a high wall this mansion has! The old gardener's footsteps from behind the wall. In the morning, he waters the flowerbeds, in the late afternoon he waters the plane and dwarf box trees at the edge of the sidewalk's water channel. Then there are white fences and hanging purple clusters, then the gable-roofed stone mansion, and then the mansion of sweetbriers.

Behind the fence, I grasp the bars of the gate — ahead of me is green; overhead, blue. The mansion is not very big. Several rooms downstairs and two rooms and one terrace upstairs. It's open from three directions and attached to the garage from the fourth side. Its west and south run alongside flowerbeds. Its north opens to a small front yard separated from the lane by fences and sweetbriers. A narrow stone path surrounding the house leads to a vast veranda with a staircase. The shiny newborn leaves of magnolia here and there among decorative palms, bunches of yellow and red tulips, Japanese blossoms, violets at the edge of the veranda, the western wall covered by ivy, on the other side across from me the fence full of morning glory leaves. During the month the flower blooms, I can take the side lane down to their fence to stretch a hand through it and touch softly, secretly that thin blue-purple skin with my fingertips. The morning room has three bright windowed sides and one shady side. If I turn my head left, I can easily see inside. The curtains are parted. The breakfast table's set. The old man always sits facing the east. He tucks a while napkin into his collar — I know that. The thin skin, white hair, clean shirt, narrow tie, and ... curved back. I hear the sound of the teaspoon stirring a cup of sweetened tea. The revolving sprinklers have just been turned on. The lawn isn't drenched yet.

Every morning the lady of the house meanders in her small garden and turns on the sprinklers. The old man eats his breakfast slowly. He doesn't pay attention to his surroundings. His jaws move slowly — I know that. The lady of the house softly appears around the curve of the veranda. Slim and tall. Her styled short hair is the colour of straw and amber. Her black silk house robe has big orange flowers.

Going on, I look up. The boughs frame the sun. Sounds vanish. The sound of sparrows remains. Having reached the end of the lane, I pause to take a breath. Not a good idea to walk on the street. I take a taxi. The sunlight dazzles me. I turn my head. Next to me, a healthy-looking young man; next to him, an apparent vendor with a brownish-maroon Samsonite made in Taiwan. The driver smiles and turns on the radio: *Hi! Good morning to you! Dear citizen, wake up, open up like a flower! Look at the spring that's come to our city and brought us joy and freshness and greenness and pinkness and passion and happiness and delight and sweetness ...may Homa, the Prosperity Bird, be above your head!... I like you a lot, my fellow countryman ... Here is the season of flower and lily and jasmine ... The angel will come ... The angel will come ... The angel will come ... "*

"Please stop here! How much should I pay?"

"Whatever you like, sister."

I give him a bill. He gives me change, steps on the gas, and speeds away.

The office's garden is quiet, the Judas trees in a line. Clumps of flowers like large and small colourful fists over the trunks.

I open my office door. I sit at the new white table. I stare at a small bouquet of freesia in yellow and purple and fuchsia with a yellowish green ribbon and a golden-rimmed white card. So, my dear co-worker hasn't forgotten my birthday!

A bird perches on the windowsill. I look at it closely: a long black tail, a grey chest, and a narrow white ring around the eyes. While singing, it holds its head up; when silent, it pecks at the glass.

## II

My husband rubs the foamy shaving brush over his face with a cadenced movement. I cannot see his profile.

"What a strange time to shave!

He doesn't hear me. I see one of his eyes, widened, in a corner of the mirror. I take off the maqna'eh and throw it on a clothes hanger.

"How come you're back so soon?"

"I took a few hours off."

He whistles:

"Why?"

"We've been invited to a party tonight."

I take off the manteau without unbuttoning all the way. His left eyebrow moves up in the mirror:

"Where?"

"At Lady Auntie's daughter's. You're invited too. You're coming. Aren't you?" Lady Auntie is my mother's older sister.

His left eyebrow moves down and goes up:

"If I can... maybe... don't wait for me."

Somebody knocks. The left eyebrow moves down:

"Are you going to answer the door?"

I press the button to release the door. My son enters, grinning. He lifts his hand:

"Look what I've brought for you!"

The foamy face of my husband peeps out.

"Your report card?"

"Yes."

Our son comes to me. His fine white skin flushes. His bright hazel eyes. He licks his pinkish lips. I stretch to grab the green sheet. I take a quick look. What a relief.

"Well done!"

It seems that he doesn't hear me. He looks as if he wants to hear something more. I stare at his new line of moustache.

## III

"What a stylish spring suit you're wearing!"

I smile and nod. I touch my pressed white skirt. Lady Auntie's daughter keeps making compliments. The courtyard isn't big; it has a wooden arbour, flowerbeds, and a tiled pool though. The white chairs are set around the arbour. The clamour from the kids mingles with guests' babble and the loud old record-player. Lady Auntie yanks her new hearing aid out and furiously throws it on the ground. The son-in-law of Dame Aunt, my father's sister, tells jokes non-stop in a circle of women laughing non-stop. Her husband plays backgammon with his brother-in-law on the veranda. The noise of their boasts as they play penetrates the honeysuckle leaves and reaches me. The twin girls of Dear Uncle, my mother's brother, wear identical shiny yellow dresses. They offer cake and ice cream with strawberries. When they stoop, their big hoop earrings clatter. The daughter of Lady Auntie pats her styled hair-streaked blonde. She pouts her lips. Dear Uncle links his squat white fingers. He leans his wrists against his big belly. He moves his head right and left. Domineering, he says:

"Well, why are you stretching it out? Tell us the rest of the story!"

The sister-in-law of Lady Auntie's daughter, who's still laughing at the joke told by the son-in-law of Dame Aunt, pulls her chair forward. She waves her hand and says:

"What's your hurry? Let her tell the story from the start..."

The younger daughter of Dear Auntie interrupts her:

"It's not a funny story."

The sister-in-law of the daughter of Lady Auntie gives her a dirty look:

"So, what is it?"

The younger daughter of Dear Auntie shrugs:

"It's a true story."

Lady Auntie's daughter shows her arms laden with golden bracelets:

"Well, as I said before, my niece got married recently and..."

Dear Auntie 's younger daughter butts in:

"She's a lucky bride. Ask her how she could snag a goldsmith husband, maybe I can too..."

The sister-in-law of Lady Auntie's daughter bursts out laughing. Dear Uncle frowns. Lady Auntie's daughter says:

"My brother's son-in-law is perfect..."

Dear Auntie's younger daughter doesn't let her finish:

"He's young, handsome, rich, and..."

Dear Uncle gives her a dirty look. Lady Auntie's daughter says:

"Oh, yeah!... Anyway, the newly married bride groom offers the bride a golden bracelet as a New Year's present. What a bracelet!"

Dear Auntie 's younger daughter can't help saying:

"Good for her!"

"... Then it gets lost. They search the house and the car, but they can't find it. Finally, they give up. But my brother's son-in-law, who happens to be very brainy, tells the story to the nearby goldsmith so he can keep his eyes open..."

The husband of Lady Auntie's daughter turns on the veranda's fluorescent light. The twins of Dear Uncle take in trays to collect plates and ice cream bowls. The sister-in-law of Lady Auntie's daughter pats my arm:

"So, why didn't your husband come to the party?"

I turn to her. Dear Uncle's twins say together: "Oops! Your skirt stained!"

## IV

She had fallen asleep. If the white skirt of her spring suit hadn't been stained, she wouldn't have awakened. Now she closes her eyes. It's useless. She doesn't see it: the same eternal mosquito — half-circling around her head from one shoulder to the other, buzzing in this ear, silence, buzzing in another ear. The artificial fragrance of the insect repellent makes her nose itch. As if the mosquito revives from this smell — the artificial version of a wildflower. Nervously she shifts her head. It's useless. She turns to the wall. The corner between the wall and bed is darker. She pulls the rough blanket over her face. She clenches her fists and presses them between her knees. She tucks her legs into her belly. The pleasant warmth and dark aren't enough. She should sink more. She should get lost. She closes her eyes tighter. A thick sticky darkness. So, she had seen a movie — a visual story. Dear Auntie's younger daughter had said, "audio," but it had become visual in her dream. The movie watcher had sunk into darkness. The people in the movie had been bright. A young couple, the handsome, the happy... Homa, the symbol of prosperity, had flapped wings ... their car was a Jeep, *"deer of the desert and bride of the street"*... the New Year holiday trip... when Dear Auntie's younger daughter had whispered that the actor was a goldsmith, Lady Auntie's daughter frowned and grumbled that he represented all the goldsmiths of all the gold-rich provinces of the country... then the newly married bride came strutted up grinning to show off her bracelet to each member of the audience. What a golden glow, what a sweet smile. Then suddenly the movie turned black and white. A poor woman seemed to walk in ashes. When she stumbled, Dear Auntie's younger daughter loudly said, "Oops! What a golden glow, pick it up!' She picked it up. Dear Auntie's younger daughter giggled in the dark. The poor woman couldn't believe it at first. The actor didn't turn a hair when he learned that the girl had lost the bracelet. He just said something to the neighbourhood goldsmith. The squat fingers of the shop-owner played with his double chin, "This bracelet you want to sell isn't yours, lady. It belongs to someone. Return it and get a reward!" The poor woman blushed, "Shame on you, accusing someone who could be your mother!" Between fingers, the man's double chin stretched. "When you're taken before the Conflict

Committee, they'll curb your tongue. They know how to make you confess." When the actor put the bracelet on the girl's wrist, the movie turned Technicolor again. What a nonsensical dream! The stain on the white skirt of her spring suit wasn't all melting ice cream. The person who's been showing the bracelet to the audience wasn't the girl, but Lady Auntie's daughter. Dear Uncle's twin girls, with their identical phosphorous yellow dresses and big hoop earrings, had come forward. However, the warm sticky ice cream had dropped from the gold-covered arm of Lady Auntie's daughter. Her sister-in-law had deliberately struck her arm, saying. "So, why didn't your husband come to the party?" Her saliva had sprayed her face. She'd been sure that he wouldn't go to the party, but not because he didn't like a big dinner, or playing backgammon, or banal conversation and unfunny jokes. But it's not certain that it was the mosquito that had awakened her, or her husband's snoring. He has his back to her, his face to the wall. His snoring isn't that loud. The stain was not really so noticeable. She hasn't seen the mosquito. So, then this annoying buzzing... She angrily squeezes her eyelids tight. She has to sink more — into the ground, under the stone and the soil. But how can she be sure that she'd be safe there? The foamy profile gradually appears. Certainly, he hadn't said, "Are you going to answer the

door?" The left eyebrow had moved down. He'd said,
"Are you going to answer the door or not?" Her arms
and legs are numb. She doesn't toss and turn. She pulls
the rough blanket over her head. She's short of breath
because of the stale air. She hears her son speaking
vaguely and brokenly from his bedroom across the hall.
He's restless, but no more restless than she is. The thin
white skin, pink lips. She stares at the bright hazel eyes
of the boy. He has lied to his mother. She's ready to
forgive him. She doesn't take her eyes off him. Her look
pleads, "Be sorry, please be sorry! At least please don't
tell lies to your mother!' The thin white skin blushes. He
licks pink lips. The bright eyes have dulled. It's useless.
She sees the new line of moustache above his mouth and
lowers her head. From now on it's not necessary to rush
to his bedroom across as soon as she hears a word or a
moan or a quick breath. The invisible mosquito doesn't
give up. A buzzing in this ear, silence, buzzing in the
other ear. The mosquito doesn't leave her alone. She
opens her fists. She pulls away the blanket. She covers
her ears with her palms. Who is the little bird singing to?
It doesn't sing. It moans, not on the windowsill but
down there in the grass. Down there, the little bird with
a long tail and a grey chest has fallen. White around its
eyes, and red down the middle of its head. Among the
needles of the old pine in the opposite side crows make

their croaking laughter. So maybe the stain on the white skirt of her spring suit was red. Her dear co-worker throws the withered bouquet of freesia in yellow and purple and the fuchsia at her chest and bursts into laughter. A small bouquet of flowers, a small lie, a big reward. The mosquito is small enough to go into her ear, if it wants, and big enough to fill her skull. She becomes delirious. The hands of the time clock speed. The black letters of the notice about new office regulations warp: *In the near future the new building will be vacated and employees will be returned to the old building.* She feels anxious. She's out of breath. Her arms and legs feel pins and needles. She doesn't have enough room. She'd looked at herself confusedly. She's as slim as always. The big young guy next to her hasn't been fat either. The apparent marketer with the Samsonite briefcase made in Taiwan had been so small that she wondered how he could carry its heavy weight. So why is her room so cramped? She presses her legs together. She has been sitting so close to the door that she could have been tossed outside at any moment. She has been thinking about speaking up. She has taken a quick look at the driver's mirror. Even once she gave the man next to him a dirty look. The big young guy has relaxed his big legs and sprawled. The small apparent marketer has been sitting relaxed. She's been crowded in. Her forehead gets sweaty because of the pressure of doubt about whether to say something. The mosquito buzzes in her ear. That's right. She always reaches her destination without protesting. The echo of the singer's deep voice has been cracking her skull. The driver has been nodding to the sound of the radio. When he said, "Whatever you like, sister," a friendly smile stayed on the corner of his lips. She counts the change. The driver has taken double fare. Nonetheless, she told herself that it was because of the U.S. dollar rate. The mosquito doesn't leave her alone. The sound of sparrows has gone away. Sounds remain. A shot from the Colonel's garden. Her heart starts beating madly. The ground under her feet has been trembling. The sound of a drill grows closer. They've been digging the asphalt, demolishing the garden lane, frightening mice. The old gardener is putting a mousetrap on the edge of the stream between the rows of plane trees as well as between the dwarf box trees. If she peeps out, she'll see the anxious mice. Her place has become tight — dark and tight. In the daylight the newly awakened disabled veterans are coming out of the gable-roofed stone mansion in a line — they are taking a morning outing in their shiny brand-new wheelchairs. She reaches the mansion of sweetbriers. She stretches her hand — the pale light of flowers. The lady of the house, with her back to her, disappears around the corner of the veranda. So, hasn't the hand of the old man turned the teaspoon in the cup of tea? The revolving sprinklers are off. Every morning, the lady of the house... her body has been stayed cold — cold and dark. The mansion collapses. She doesn't see it – the same eternal mosquito.

# THE YELLOW STATION

## I

Sari on the Caspian Sea, warm drizzle, the yellow train station. Pairs of glasses with white plastic arms and lenses of coloured mica. Through the red lens the station is orange. Through the blue ones it's green. Through the ... Oh! Shafigheh spreads her little hands. The cheap plastic glasses dangle from her fingers. She looks up. She lifts her face to the rain. She runs into the wet quiet street. She yells, "They all belong to me!" Mother runs after her. She grabs her collar and yanks her back. Mother says angrily, "What are you doing? Don't you see that it's the street?' *I look at Mother, not indignant, but confused.* Mother looks like a stranger. Whenever Mother refuses her request or quarrels with her, she becomes a stranger. Shafigheh now walks slowly along the curb. She spreads her little hands again. She looks up. She lifts her face to the raindrops. She says softly, "They all belong to me!" Cousin can't hide his annoyance. He says, "Are you talking about glasses?"

His voice sounds dry and sharp because he's jealous. *I shouldn't answer him right away.* "'My son's naïve. All his friends pick on him. Maybe he's too soft-hearted..." It was Aunt's voice. Dazed, Shafigheh turns her head. When Cousin first arrived, he looked friendly. He'd deceived her once again. She'd brought along all her toys. Her cousin took them all; he handled them so much he ruined them. When Shafigheh wanted to protest, he frowned and turned his back to her. *I tried to keep my mouth shut. Not because I was afraid of him.* "He's our guest. He's your cousin. If you want to play, you shouldn't complain." But it's not fair that he takes all the toys and just orders her around. Again, it is Mother's voice. "Now that you've found a playmate, you should get along with him; otherwise, you'll be alone again." She'd rather be alone. She's afraid of darkness, the toilet at the end of the courtyard, the dogs and cows in the vacant lot. But she isn't afraid of loneliness. Cousin showed her his marbles, but he didn't let her touch them. *Why should I remain silent?*

The station was far away. On the way he'd constantly showed off his coloured glasses. He took one of its arms between his two fingers and swung the glasses in the air. Then he put them on, enjoying them, turning his head from side to side.

"Can I wear your glasses?"

She didn't hear him answer.

"Just once! I'll give them back right away."

Again she didn't hear a reply. She said to herself, "Damn it!' Her eyes become full of tears. Grandma was in a rush. However, as soon as she came to a variety store, she stopped. Mother said:

"Aren't you in a rush because you think you might be late?"

Having taken Shafigheh's hand and pulled her, Grandma murmured, "Sweetie, how many glasses do you want?"

*I looked at her, confused.*

"Sir, how many of these glasses do you have?"

"Four, madam."

"Please give me all of them!" Turning to her, Grandma continued, "All of them are for you, sweetie. Don't give any of them to that mean boy! They're all yours."

The soft white plastic arms, the colourful mica. The red one: orange station. The blue one: green station. The... She turns her head. Cousin is still staring at her, waiting for a reply.

"What did you say?"

Cousin angrily yells, "I said are you talking about the glasses?"

Shafigheh smiles. She wants to have the same mysterious malicious smile as her cousin. *But my smile is joyous.* She softly says, "I'm talking about the stations." Cousin makes a face. He shrugs. He turns his head and thrusts his glasses into his pants' pocket.

Grandma is a guest. They are going with her to the station. Grandma has to take the train to go back to Tehran. Cousin is a guest too. In one or two days he'll go back to his hometown too. Then Shafigheh will be alone with Mother and the town, with rain and the colourful mica lenses and the yellow station. *I miss Grandma very much.*

On the sidewalk under the silk trees, they were coming back from the house of the town's governor. Mother's hands were warm; damp hands. Nazila was her classmate. She was not home. The governor's wife wasn't home either. Nazila's grandmother said, "Come in, please!" She said that just once. Mother went in right away. The room was big; it was spacious and sunlit. The easy chair was of patterned satin fabric, soft and floral. She had rubbed her hands gently over the arm of her seat. Mother was nervously watching her. Mother had shrunk. Mother had sunk into her seat. Nazila's grandmother was tall and elegant; styled grey hair and pince-nez. She had liked Mother's sewing. They had been offered ice cream; vanilla ice cream with cherries and sweet biscuits. The crystal dish shone. She had swallowed quietly. The glass was round, with a tall, narrow, transparent stem. She gently rubbed her fingers over the cold crystal. The thin suit of Nazila's grandmother was grey, well-pressed.

Grandma's black chador had got wrinkled. Grandma's hair under it had been unkempt. Grandma had become small. If she hadn't seen Nazila's grandmother, she would have jumped into Grandma's bosom. She wiped the trace of Grandma's juicy kiss off her cheek with the back of her hand. Nazila's grandmother had shaken hands with Mother. When Mother had spoken to Grandma, she'd muttered in response to. But Grandma was saying nice words to Nazila's grandmother non-stop. Shafigheh had got annoyed.

The rain comes quicker. It stitches sky and earth. It's like the big and small stitches on the silk dress of the governor's wife. *I look up. The stitches dissolve. I don't see the soft hanging pink and white clusters of the silk tree above my head.* The yellow station swells. She holds Grandma's hand under the damp black chador. Cousin, frowning, passes the shiny wet hedges. He drags his right palm along them. *I sympathize with him.* On the other side of the hedges the wooden blind of a room's window opens. The small lamp hanging from the ceiling shines yellow. A young man appears in the window frame. He holds a big accordion. He doesn't look at the garden, or the street, or the sky and its rain.

The puffy sleeves of his shirt mildly tremble to the quick movement of his fingers on the keys. Shafigheh becomes depressed. Like little grey birds, the notes fly disturbed out of the window frame. Under the colourless drizzle, in fog, they vanish. *Grandma lets go of my hand.*

Breath fogs the cold glass. A cold draft from the snow seeps in. *I erase the mist on the window with my frozen fingertips.* The damp brick paving of the courtyard, the overcast sky, the big empty pool, the tired pine. The room is heavy with Grandma's laboured breaths. She's lying on her back; her hands spread across her painful chest. Sometimes she opens her puffy eyelids and stares at the high white ceiling. Sometimes her swollen dark lips move. Her harsh voice has deepened. She is talking to herself. Why does the sky itself become heavy? The heaviness of infected lungs is unbearable. Her arms and legs have grown limp. This cracked ceiling doesn't have the plaster tulips and big pale roses her ceiling once had.

*Outside it's snowing, gently and quietly. I imagine an old woman beyond the slanting white curtain; she has a bad bladder and a scratchy memory. She sits under the pine and strikes a match. She strikes the matches and burns sheets of papers one by one. She pushes back the curtain of snow with trembling hands.*

It's so high! Shafigheh is sitting on the edge of the high veranda. She restlessly jiggles her legs:

"Shall I jump?"

Nobody replies. Grandma sits next to samovar with her legs crossed. She is listening to the water bubbling.

"Shall I jump?"

Father is reading the newspaper. Mother is going and coming. Mother is going and coming and doesn't look at her.

"Grandma, shall I jump?"

Grandma smiles:

"If you're not afraid, jump!"

"Will I break my arms and legs if I jump?"

"If you're afraid, you'll break your arms and legs."

Shafigheh asked:

"Why shouldn't I jump?"

Mother frowned.

"Just look at how far below it is! You'll break your arms and legs."

"But you always jump, so why are you afraid for me?"

"I'm afraid in case you break your arms and legs."

"Grandma says I can jump if I'm not afraid.

Mother mumbles:

"She doesn't care about you."

"Grandma is not afraid."

"She's afraid. Have you ever seen her jump from this height?"

She hasn't seen that. Grandma greatly fears doomsday and hell. Grandma had said so. That's why Grandma never delays her daily prayers. Grandma is also afraid of Aqa, Grandpa. "Grandma is very afraid of Aqa," Mother had said quietly so Father doesn't hear. She had seen Aqa. He wasn't frightening at all. He had unfastened the green shawl around his waist and wrapped it around her waist; he had chased her around the court yard. He had also carried her on his shoulders; he had taken her for a walk on the street; he had bought her halvah.

"Aqa, you're spoiling this kid."

"She should learn that her grandfather is not a monster, the way some people tell her he is."

Father blushed. He had looked down. Aqa had laughed loudly. Shafigheh had become frightened.

Shafigheh asked:

"Grandma, tell me, is the monster's laugh scary?"

"Oh, my God! Why are you asking such odd questions?"

Grandma wouldn't argue if she didn't want to. You could ask her another question. The sky was full of stars. The glare of the green light on the mosque's minaret dazzled her. The smell of moist soil on the flat roof, the coolness of the thin bed sheet, the pleasant night breeze, the sweetness of a candy cane, Grandma's voice full of regret, and... the charming tale of the Fairy King's daughter.

"Grandma, tell me if Aqa is worse than the snakes of hell?"

"Oh, my God... who are you talking about?"

"Did I upset you?"

"Oh, sweetie, it's just that you're so nosy!"

"Is it a sin to be nosy?"

"Oh, no. Children are innocent. I'll tell you, I'll say it just to you."

Mother goes and comes. *Why should I have been afraid?*

"So, I'll jump."

Mother goes and comes. Mother doesn't look at her, but growls:

"No, you won't!"

Granny wrinkles her forehead in a frown.

Father said:

"Don't quarrel with this kid when my mother is here. It upsets her."

Mother flushed with anger. She muttered:

"Why did she abandon you, her only child, if she's so kind-hearted?"

"Again, you started to squabble!"

"Aren't I right? A baby isn't like a dowry. You can't give it away like money. A woman who abandons her child to save herself isn't a mother..."

"You're the only mother on the earth, I know."

"If I wasn't a mother, I couldn't tolerate you."

As always, it is Mother who starts squabbling and ends up crying.

As always, she loses her fear by staring at the brick paving below, yet she doesn't jump in order not to annoy Mother. They hear a knock on the door. Mother says:

"Run and open the door!"

When she reaches the corridor, she hears Father saying:

"Hold on! I'll open the door."

Grandma's swollen dark lips move.

"Do you want anything?"

She nods:

"Someone's knocking."

"No, it's just snowing."

"For you, it's snowing. For me, it's the Angel of Death coming for me."

Grandma turns her face away.

"Grandma, you don't like me anymore, do you?"

"When you get to the point I have, you won't like anybody anymore, sweetie. I've gotten detached. What do you expect from me?"

Father is nervous. He lingers. Aqa smiles:

"Why are you surprised? Let me come in. I'm dead tired.

Father says loudly:

"Shafigheh, run and let them know that Aqa has arrived!"

She runs as fast as the wind. Mother's white complexion gets paler. Grandma's dark skin gets purple. Grandma, calling on saints for help, runs into the room. Mother rushes after her:

"What are you going to do?"

"I'm going to hide myself in the closet and stay there as long as he's here."

"At least don't close the door completely! We'll try to get rid of him. He won't come inside the room."

Grandma says furiously:

"I don't want to see him. That wounded snake will get around to stinging me."

Shafigheh stands confused on the verandah, staring at Aqa, who's approaching suspiciously, suspecting that his former wife may be inside.

Shafigheh asked:

"You didn't like Aqa. Did you?"

"In our day they didn't ask girls if they were interested in marrying someone or not, let alone such things. One day they said a guy named Sayyed Heydar had arrived in the neighbourhood. Then my mother said, 'Don't go to school any more! You've got enough education. I've sworn that you'll marry Sayyed.'..." Sayyed was a descendent of the Prophet.

Grandma started coughing. She bent forward and held the bowl of water in her hands.

"Was Aqa a bad guy?"

"What an odd question, sweetie! One shouldn't say that a Sayyed, the Prophet's descendent, is a bad guy. Well, nobody's perfect. The only perfect one is God. This Sayyed was very generous to me. He didn't beat me. He only said nice words. He had concubines, but that wasn't really his fault. It was his habit. But I wanted to be free. I wanted to be free to go wherever I liked, to do whatever I wanted. I didn't like to be afraid whether Aqa approved of what I did or didn't do. So one day I made up my mind and the next time he went on a trip, I sold all the furniture to a second-hand dealer, I took the baby to his grandmother to take care of him, and I ran away. I went to the Holy Ma'sumeh Shrine and took refuge there in case he came to cut my throat. God helped me. Finally, his anger subsided. Well, I was innocent... he's threatened me a lot, though..."

Shafigheh asked:

"Grandma, are you afraid to die?"

*I don't say that loudly. Grandma won't reply even if she hears me. The courtyard's brick pavement is covered in white. It's not snowing anymore. The old woman under the pine still burns the sheets of paper one by one. Breaths fog the cold glass.*

Grandma's swollen dark lips move:

"Sayyed Heydar, you've come!"

Legs, legs grow heavy and heavier. A clotted warmth covers her Grandma's legs and makes them limp. Why can't she make them walk? Why can't they make her walk? Grandma's eyelids are closed. *The tableau is so close that it dims the vision. Oh, God, I'm not old yet!*

Shafigheh asked:

"What do old people think about?"

"Old people? I don't think that they think at all."

"So what do they do?"

"They see. They see a long way ahead."

She feels that her mother's stitches have sewn her to the earth.

"My fingertips are all pins and needles because I work with needles."

"Why do you sew so much? Father's coming soon. Why do you sew so much for everybody?"

"I just sew for you. When will you grow up enough to understand this?"

Shafigheh's sister smirks. Shafigheh looks down, upset. She says to herself, "It's as if you're sewing me."

*Legs, closed legs, stitched legs; heavy legs, with no energy to move. These legs don't move; don't go ahead; don't take me ahead. God, I'm stuck.*

Mother said:

"I can't go ahead or go back. My God, what the hell should I do?"

"Mother, how many times do you say this? How many days, how many years?"

Mother doesn't reply. She moans softly and quietly weeps.

"Well, why don't you leave the house? You can go, like Grandmother!"

"Where shall I go? How can I leave you alone and go? How can I ignore my children? Now you're telling me to go. But you don't tell me where to go.

When I was young, and you were just a little kid, you said something different..."

*I didn't say anything. I just looked at her, and my gaze was so heavy that it didn't allow her to go.*

Shafigheh's sister hid in the closet, or backyard, or the empty water tank in the basement. She did this because she was very afraid of Father's anger, and she hated Mother's weeping and moaning. Shafigheh didn't approach Mother. Though her mother didn't go away. Her knees started to shiver. But she was not afraid of Father. She was never afraid of him. Maybe that was why Father never spanked her. Shafigheh's sister was afraid. She was afraid of spanking, of Father, of Mother's anger, of being left alone. Shafigheh was not afraid of loneliness. If Mother had left them alone, she would have been upset. Not because her mother wasn't there, but because she knew her mother would be lonely without them.

"If Mother leaves us, we'll have a stepmother."

"There's nothing wrong with a stepmother."

"So why are you crying if she isn't a dreadful person?"

"I'm crying because Mother is crying."

She's crying. She's pressing her back to the wall. She's clamping her knees together. Her thighs are restless. She welds her thighs together and squeezes. She squeezes them together but it's no good: they're wet. Her hands aren't numb yet, though she's been clutching Mother's breast and belly. She doesn't say a word, but constantly tells herself, "You shouldn't go! You shouldn't go!" Father is about to launch another attack. Mother is weeping, screaming, cursing. Grandma stands in the doorway. Not looking at anyone, she says, "Well, even if you really want to leave, do it after our guests leave!" Mother becomes silent. Shafigheh's hands on Mother's belly relax. Mother presses Shafigheh against her breast. Shafigheh curls her arms around Mother's waist. The warmth of Mother's belly, the saltiness of tears, the heavy boughs of the cherry tree, the hot bitter wind.

She rolls down the car window. A hot bitter wind hurtles in. She breathes deep the smoky air. The sound of motors and the street noise obscure Father's words. She stares ahead. She doesn't want to look at Father's face. *Why am I afraid of that?* Father complains. He is complaining about Mother. She hears every other word, some of them repeated. Even when not said or repeated, the words remain heard. "It's good that he's driving," she says to herself. The traffic is heavy. The smoky hot weather of a summer night heavily oppresses her. The words are heavy: "When she was young, she wasn't like that. It's as if now she's taking revenge. She doesn't care that I'm old. She nags, nags, nags all the time."

*I look ahead at the red light. I sympathize with Father. Yet this isn't the father who keeps me here. God, what tie has bound me to the past? Grandma flees; she runs away. She runs away; she flees. Her eyes are riveted on her back, though. I don't want to see my own back.*

Shafigheh said:

"I don't know why I fall down so much."

"That's because you're absent-minded, sweetie. You're not focused. You're puzzled.

Shafighteh's sister smiles. Her sweet smile isn't hurtful:

"Look in front of you!"

*Do I look ahead of me? I'm not afraid of what lies behind me, but I cannot run. My knees feel feeble. I don't move forward. Or maybe I do.*

Mother said:

"How do you dare say that you want to marry this underprivileged lad! If your father learns that..."

Shafigheh is not afraid of Mother. The louder Mother yells, the bolder she gets. She lets Mother curse, cry, blame her. Finally, she stands and says gently:

"I said I will marry him, and I will. It doesn't matter whether you like it or not."

Mother's complexion becomes bloodless. Shafigheh doesn't linger. She leaves her room and home. So she can comfort herself that sometimes, only sometimes, she's stepped forward. Or perhaps she's stepped backward. Back or forth, she's moved.

Her husband said:

"Let's go! Let's get out of here! Now that you've cut off your family, what are you waiting for? If we stay here, sooner or later, we'll be trapped. You know that."

Shafigheh, bored, turns her face away from her husband:

"I know that. But I'm not going anywhere. Why should we flee? Didn't you know that you'd have to pay the price if you wanted to be a dissident?"

"Stop it! That's enough."

Enough. The sky and earth has turned the colour of hypocrisy. The smell of it tries to escape; it cracks the skin trying to get out.

Mother had become withered. Her eyes watered, her lips cracked, her thin white skin wrinkled, the blue veins of her slender hands... *Oh, I moved ahead. Apparently I moved ahead. Or I wanted to move ahead. Why do you, Mother, pull me back?*

Shafigheh's sister smiles. Her smile is enigmatic, not bitter:

"You weren't scared because of Father's appalling presence, or because of Mother's quarrels. You followed your own way. But now it's different. I know your weakness. If someone attacks you, he'll lose for sure. Mother made the same mistake that Father did. Whenever you face force, you get strong, then nobody can defeat you. If your rival's stronger than you, you'll make him give up. But when you face someone who's weaker than you, then..."

"Stop it, for God's sake, that's enough."

Shafigheh said:

"Mother, please stop it, for God's sake, that's enough."

Mother holds the baby in her arms tightly and without thinking pats her back. She doesn't stop, though:

"You're not a child anymore. You've become a mother, but still you don't want to be wise. Did you produce this baby for my lap? When will you give up these political ideas and activities? You suffer to bring up a child and eventually you realize that you don't have any control. Now you expect that control of world can go to you and people like you..."

"That's enough, Mother. You know that I do whatever I want."

"But that's the way the world has been from the beginning, always and everywhere, and that's what it's going to be like this in the future. That's the rule: you overpower others, or they overpower you. There's nothing in between, my dear," Father says.

"But I say that it's not that simple. The one who gets overpowered may not get that way forever but even if he does, he'll somehow retaliate ..."

Shafigheh didn't say aloud, "So, Father, now you're so helpless that you're liable to walk into a wall. Now... now I feel sorry for you."

Shafigh's sister, bored, had said:

"You always feel sorry for someone, if not for Mother, or this person or that person, then for the birds in the sky or for the fish in the sea..."

"But you didn't see how Father slammed Mother's head into the wall."

Shafigheh's sister had paused and then shrugged her shoulders:

"Well, Mother swore at him. So he fought back."

The police captain's wife was tall and stout and dark-skinned and thick-lipped. Her eyes, though, were hazel; and when she was not angry or overbearing, her eyes smiled. Mother said:

"But he doesn't know about that. If I come to the movie theatre with you..."

Standing in front of her, looking up, Shafigheh feels the laughter of the captain's wife wash over her. The captain's wife was not afraid of anybody. She ordered all the policemen around. She gave the captain orders. She ordered Mother around too:

"Let's go! I told the cop Ahmadi to buy us tickets. You aren't scared to ask for your husband's permission, are you?"

The scent of roasted nuts, the neon lights, the wide cement staircase of the movie theatre, the huge bright posters, the long red polished nails of the captain's wife.

At midnight Mother had moaned:

"But every night you go out to have a good time and come home late. It wasn't a sin to take your kids to the movies. Do you ever ask me or tell me when you go out ..."

Shafigheh had murmured:

"How is that the captain heeds his wife?"

"Well, the captain's wife is stronger than the captain. She has fingernails like a leopardess."

*Father could go wherever he liked and do whatever he liked. Mother couldn't. That's it. That's what ties me up to the past. Mother cannot and with her*

*lack of ability weighs me down, ties me down. God help*
*me, I'll never be free of it.*

## II

*Love was red. I still remember its colour. The desert sun*
*burned the skin. Drops of sweats were running down my*
*forehead, trickling over ears, down my neck, settling on*
*my chest. My lips were chapped, burning.*

She's burning inside and outside. She turns the
car's window down. Sitting in the back seat, she looks at
the nape of the two men's necks: one is red, the other
olive. Both men hunched. Both of them, ignoring her
stony presence, are chatting. What the heck is she doing
here? The light gentle breeze doesn't help her breathe.
Dust plugs her nostrils. She starts sneezing. The noise of
the junk heap swallows the sound of her sneezes. The
side mirror is cracked and dusty. She digs a piece of a
broken mirror out of the hot plastic bag next to her. She
wants to see if any breath comes out or not. She eats, she
sleeps; she goes, she comes; it seems to her that she
doesn't breathe, though. What air can she inhale? What
flower can she smell? For a moment, the sweet scent of
her little daughter revives softly in her mind. It comes
like a breeze from the farthest, coolest, bluest corner of
the sky; it passes over her crumpled body and soul and

goes to the farthest, coolest, bluest other corner of the sky. She becomes upset.

Her husband had said:

"We'll take the baby with us?"

"To that hot place?"

"The desert's nights are cool."

She said:

"I won't take the baby."

And the man was reluctantly forced to agree. For her part, the woman had backed up a step and agreed to go. Maybe the woman could make the man realize that a dance requires both partners to move together, one step forward, one step back. A compromise. If they couldn't do that, no one would win and eventually there'd be two losers.

*The sweat rains on me, a warm rain, a warm drizzle and... I don't remember any more. Muggy skin, dry mouth, a bitter taste in my mouth, cracked lips but, despite it, all this is the desert that I've loved. I should remember. The tableau doesn't have any frame – an unlimited landscape which loses all colour in the streaming light. This sun doesn't know hypocrisy. It strips everything naked and burns. Now I only remember its redness, and as yet I can't remember what else I don't remember yet what was calling me.*

The water streams down. She'd held the little cold globe of the cold-water tap in her fist, constantly turning it to make the water colder. Cold water could dampen her anger. She had to make a decision. She shouldn't yield and obey. She should get out of the marriage. If the man won't divorce her... all she has to do is turn off the tap, dry herself, get dressed, leave home; and never, ever come back. She can go somewhere far from here, even further than she wants... All of a sudden her fist unclenches. Cold water still pours. She is freezing. As if her ears are becoming increasingly open. A sound attacks her, the sound of a gentle, innocent weeping. She tightly shuts her eyes, but she can still see the little girl's eyes, though — the look in those amber almond-shaped eyes. She could see those lips — trembling lips wet with tears. Oh, God! Her daughter's calling her. She is calling her. She is calling her.

Sad, she leans against the wall. Sitting under the green umbrella of foliage, she stretches her legs over a wooden cot they've moved outside to use as a bench. The light sky of Mahan, the city at the edge of the desert, remains a tranquil nocturne. Between her palms she holds the cool porcelain bowl of *Paludeh*, the starch noodles in syrup, mixed with crushed ice, flavoured with rose water. Without caring what they say, she hears men chatting. Their host half reclines next to the apparatus for smoking opium. He, Rostam Khan, unlike Rostam the hero, is small and feeble. However, he has an impressive moustache, and his look retains traces of the old days in which he was a feudal lord. His follower sits on his knee. He is neither Rostam Khan's butler nor valet. He is one of the band of tough guys of a neighbourhood, bullies in the name of order of the area, keeping solidarity among themselves. He is young, chivalrous in his way. He is Rostam Khan's friend, companion, and fellow opium-smoker. He still practices *varzesh-e bastani*, the ancient martial art. Rostam Khan's wife brings a fruit basket. She distributes green crystal plates. She is thin and dark-skinned, her eyes burning either from regret of not producing a baby boy, or sadness at having a rival, or maybe from the smoke of a burning love. A lord with half-grey hair, puffy bags under the eyes, a drooping salt-and-pepper moustache, a gastric ulcer, chronic hemorrhoids, and a painful lower back. A teenage peasant girl with wide shoulders, big firm breasts, and a big bum might have ensured a male successor. She feels compassion for the woman, and annoyance at her weakness.

Across from her are flowerbeds: two fig trees, short, heavy, and dusty; pale petunias. Two wagtails perch on the narrow brick-paved path between two flowerbeds; they hop and fly together and disappear among the foliage. The mouth of the yellow plaster goose in the middle of the cement-lined basin is open to the sun. Her feet are stuck in the slime of the stagnant water. The soft curve of her long neck caresses the eyes. Her raised head says "No" to the stagnant water. Ghorab, the black dog, starts barking from the corner of the garden. Rostam Khan's follower swears at it. She tucks her legs under her and keeps staring at the plaster goose. She tilts up her head instinctively, as if she wants to say "No" forever. She feels the heaviness of her husband's eyes on her. She doesn't move. Suddenly her cheeks flush, bitterness rises in her throat. She turns towards him and looks at eyes, cold and glassy. She turns her head away. She remembers.

"Why math? Not all girls are good at math. Even if they could be, what would be the result? You could be a doctor, or a teacher..." said Father.

Father kept saying "No" for three months and Shafigheh kept not listening to him.

"If you want to marry this guy, you should leave my house forever!" said Father.

Shafigheh had left the house at once, maybe because Mother, who couldn't believe she would, hadn't started to weep.

Father had said, "You should find a job with the government. When I told you that it wouldn't be good for you to become an engineer, you..." Her husband had said, "We should leave the country, otherwise..." Father had said... The man had said... Father... The man... Father... The man... Shafigheh had heard all orders and hadn't obeyed any of them.

But what had Shafigheh done? Or what does she do? Or what will she do? She takes the invisible scale of the angel, lost in distant dreams, in her hands. She measures the heaviness and lightness of presences and absences; qualifications and disqualifications; strengths and weaknesses. She is obsessed with balance, making the pans of the scale equal. She makes the heavy pan light; she makes the light pan heavy. What does Shafigheh do? Does she do anything wrong?

The dog barks. Nesa, the baker, comes. Shafigheh gets up. She wants to watch Nesa while she does her task. Nesa bakes bread. She sweats and bakes bread. She wipes off the sweat on her face with the edge of her sleeves and bakes bread. She narrows her eyes and bakes bread.

"I've become too old. Well, peasant women bloom early and wither early. I went to his house when I was 12, madam," Nesa says.

"Whose house?"

"To the house of the man called 'husband'. At fifteen I had a baby in my arms. At twenty I left his house."

"Don't you want to remarry?"

"When I can make a living, what the hell is the use of a husband, madam?"

The fire in the oven blazes. It gains and loses. Shafigheh hugs her knees and puts her chin between them. The heat of the oven strikes her face. The doughy faces twist in the flames. Nesa sticks the thin round loaves into the oven's hot interior. "*Oh, we burn, oh, we scorch,* "a line of Shamlu's children's story. Yet faces don't burn.

Haj Aqa, the molla (mullah) assigned to adjudicate family conflicts, has a ball-like beard. He looks unfriendly:

"What's your problem, sister?"

"Me? I want to divorce, Haj Aqa."

"What about you, sister, you?"

"Me? I want to be paid my alimony."

"I want my dowry back."

"I want my child."

The tea man enters with a tray of cups, his face sour and puffy like leavened dough. He curses and kicks the door behind him. The glass cups of tea slop over. The secretary looks at the tea tray. He puts a pen on a notebook and yawns. The dough of his face has been leavened.

"Mother, if you think that by swearing more and more at your son-in-law it will make it harder for him, you're wrong."

The woman's son-in-law looks at the sty in the corner of the secretary's eye. He puffs cigarette smoke into the air. His face stretches. An employee shows him the *Don't smoke!* sign. The man angrily puffs for the last time. The woman averts her face from the smoke. The kid complains and pulls at her mother's lap. The woman pushes her towards the man. The kid grasps her father's knees. The woman's tears begin. The dough of her face dissolves. Her lips, her cheeks, her nose, her forehead, her chin, spill over the floor mosaic and break. The soles of the man's shoes stick to the ground.

"For God's sake, give me a solution!"

"Sister, the law says that mothers can only have the custody of their sons until they reach age two and their daughters until they reach 7."

"I want my children."

"You can't do anything about it. You'll only see them in your dreams."

"Brother, shame on you."

"Even if I die, my father will get custody of them, not you," her husband says.

"Give me a solution!"

"... Well, maybe there's *osr-o-haraj*, which means "intolerable hardship" according to Sharia. If you can prove that you can get a divorce without consent of your husband."

"What the hell is this 'osr-o-haraj'?" the husband asks.

"It means madness. It means suicide. It means tearing yourself to pieces with your teeth and your nails."

"Sister, please be patient!"

What are these butterflies looking for? The heat wave makes breathing difficult. Shafigheh sits down on the yellow mosaic staircase. Her chest burns. Her breathing has become slow and laboured:

"Why didn't you take your baby with yourself? You didn't want her?"

"I wanted my baby. He didn't let me."

"You couldn't do anything, could you?"

"I waited. Ten years later, when he gave her in marriage, I could visit her. You think that I didn't do a great job of saving my life, madam?"

"What did he do to you? He didn't give you money? Or did he beat you?"

"The only thing he did was torture me by humiliating me. He did this just because he thought that this was the only way he could be superior. "

What are the butterflies looking for in the daylight, in this breathtaking heat? Two tiny azure butterflies, or two white butterflies with black dots, or two yellow butterflies. Nesa sits and talks. She talks and bakes. Shafigheh struggles with her heavy breaths. She hugs her knees tighter. The doughy faces become crooked and curved. As if a hand is constantly kneading them. At a distance, beyond the clear glass, on the other side of the world, faces take shape. The man with the baby in his arms is standing on a roof. Far below a net is spread. The ambulance is ready. The speaker says that the family court won't change the verdict, even if the man jumps off the roof with the baby. The man doesn't know anything about "osr-o-haraj". He knows that he will have a place either in the cemetery or in an insane asylum. The man moves. For a moment Shafigheh cannot breathe. Nesa sweats. She bakes and sweats. She sweats and gets older. The fire blazes. It burns the air. The burnt air, the held breath, trembling hands, feeble legs. The little girl dreams of her mother. God, what bond, God, what bond binds me to the future?

## III

*I've been sitting here quietly on a worn-out bench with a broken leg. I'm looking ahead of me at a train that's still standing, or a train that has just started, or the empty spot where the train had left. I inhale the muggy air. The station empties and fills. People come, go, pass. Maybe nobody remains. Maybe nobody never ever remains. The wall clock is always awake. The clock's hands keep turning. I've been stuck in a massive, compressed volume of air and noisy bustle. Those who go away don't look at me. Those who talk don't hear me.*

"Don't you see? Don't you hear? Hurrah!"

Shafigheh's sister yells, leaps, jumps, laughs. Shafigheh doesn't move. She looks at her sister. Her sister says:

"At last, they've have given us permission. So, Mom, we can take a trip to Tehran with Grandma. So you let us go."

Mother was busy packing their suitcase. She wiped sweat off her high white forehead with the back of her hand:

"Your father gave the permission."

"You don't want us to go, Mom? Do you?"

Mother was tired, anxious, or impatient:

"Well, you can go and spent your summertime down there and enjoy it. I stay here and take a rest. I'll have a break."

Mother smiled. She wore a small, forced smile and stole her eyes from Shafigheh. Shafigheh feels that her legs become powerless. Shafigheh's sister wrapped her arms around Mother's neck. She was kissing Mother's hollow cheeks non-stop. Shafigheh says with exasperation:

"You're like a woodpecker."

Mother wore a forced smile again:

"You burn me out and then leave me alone."

"Would you like me not to go?"

Mother, frowned, looked at Shafigheh:

"Not go? But you want to go more than your sister. You like Tehran much more than her. Not only Tehran, but also your grandmother, and traveling."

"Even so, I can stay here."

Mother wrinkled her forehead more:

"You should go. You should go and take care of your sister. If you're together, I'll have more peace of mind. Did you hear me?"

"I heard you."

*I heard the sound of the water that was going away. I heard the sound of the wind that was passing by. I heard the odour of the scorched soil.*

"Is Tehran cloudy?" Shafigheh's sister asks.

"It's sunny."

"No rain? No sour orange? No sea? No forest?"

"It has sunshine. It has mountains. It has a zoo..."

"What else?"

"Big streets, bright lights, parks, flat roofs on the houses and mosquito nets. Double-decker buses and the Ferdowsi chain stores and escalators, Grandma and..."

Shafigheh's sister is discontented:

"Of all those things, I've only seen Grandma."

"Without Grandma, you cannot see any of these things."

Shafigheh's sister shrugged her shoulders.

"Why do you like to go to Tehran with Grandma, if you don't like her," Shafigheh asks.

"Silly question! Because I'd love to visit Tehran. You wouldn't?"

"I'd like to see Tehran. But if I didn't like Grandma, I wouldn't go with her to Tehran. But if we go, Mother will remain alone."

"So what?"

"She'll get upset. I won't come. I won't come."

"But we're not going to stay there forever. We'll come back."

"And until then?"

*Until then? Until when? The Earth turns. The water retreats. The wind comes and goes away. The soil stays and clings to her rough roots. The plant grows. The fire burns within. I smell something burning.*

"Staying in the country doesn't smell stale. It smells like burning. Did you know that?" she asks her friend.

Shafigheh's friend smiles:

"That it smells is enough."

"So, you're saying that one should flee from any smell," she says sadly.

"You know perfectly well that I've no desire to leave. I'm not leaving for others' sake. You, too, should think about it again. You cannot change anything if you stay here. When you cannot fix something, you should give up. When you cannot get something, you should go for something else. Then one day it'll come to you ..."

"When I might not want it anymore! I want something, but not just for myself, or maybe not for myself at all. That's the problem. You know what dream I had last night? I dreamed of that year of cholera in Mashhad. You remember that quarantine there. In any corner of the streets and lanes infected people were lying down. It looked like Doomsday. My legs had gotten numb. Many people had collapsed. Many people had been sitting slumped. Nobody could get out of the city without permission. I was almost suffocating from the heat wave, from the bad smell. Like now, you were urging me to leave the place. You asked me if I wasn't afraid of the needle. I felt as if I was numb. I felt nauseous. I couldn't move, though."

"Ah, your obsessions and compassions don't cause anything but sufferings. You think that it's easy for me to leave my homeland, to fly..."

"I wish you could fly tomorrow night."

Instead of using smugglers to flee the country, taking the obscure narrow path where only donkeys can pass, the dark mountain. The cold moonless sky, a heart beating with anxiety.

Shafigheh's friend lights a cigarette and smiles:

"You've heard about my donkey-riding adventure. The summer cottage was on the other side of the mountain. The path was only for donkeys, the August sunlight was hot, and we had heat rash. Boys were riding ahead. As always, I was behind. My donkey was walking at the edge of the path. I was sweating. I didn't dare look down. I was scared. My donkey was moving slowly, maybe daydreaming. All of a sudden she stopped at the very edge of the abyss... Just imagine... Then I felt two donkey legs over my shoulders — I mean, the donkey behind had mounted his mate... My goodness... My teeth were chattering with fear. I dug my nails into that poor animal's neck waiting for the male donkey to finish. Just imagine."

Shafigheh neither smiles or gets surprised, for she's heard the story many times:

"But now the story's different. You're on the edge of the abyss. This time the donkey is riding you. Now you have to wait until he finishes..."

She shuts her mouth. Shafigheh's friend crushes her clothes in the suitcase. The new story remains unfinished. "What is a homeland?' It is a cow you can milk for ever if the government lets you. It's *Bazm-e Golpa*, the private party where the famous Golpa sings. It is the Persian style cabaret. It's the Gol-o-Bolbol ice cream parlor. It's the monotone of classical Persian music. It's the disgusting smell of sewers and the fragrance of rose water. It's the dome and minaret and the *azan* call to prayer. A homeland is a dusty narrow lane in which you lost your childhood. Homeland is the lines and wrinkles of Mother.

*My mother has become old, feeble, and powerless. My mother has been ruined.*

The train comes; it stops; it goes away. People come; go; pass by. I've been glued to the worn-out bench with a broken leg, to the yellow station. On the other side of the railing, the old woman with an invisible face and trembling hands is striking a match. She is striking a match and burning sheets of papers one by one.

# EVERY ORANGE FLOWER IN SPRING

Barefoot, I go to the veranda to look at the sky. It's Friday evening. I'm alone, bored, and waiting. Far off at the edge of the horizon, small patches of cloud have arranged themselves next to each other, leaf by leaf. They look like goose feathers: slender, soft, and white. You can't count on them to bring rain. The heart of the sky, however, is dense with waves of bright overlapping clouds. They look like pleats of a bride's satin dress, the inner folds full of white large and small angels. Their faces, bodies, wings, and thick hair appear in bright shades. When they condense the downpour begins.

This morning, at dawn, it rained. The soil of the flowerbed beside the veranda is damp. The paved stone floor of the yard is clean and polished. The foliage of the sour orange tree is still wet. It's fall and the wind, smoothly passing by, touches my skin and the tree's body with its cool hand. I take a deep breath. I like the smell of damp soil, but I miss the scent of the orange flower. My orange tree has flowered seven times so far. The first one was the springtime when Zahra Jan came to our home.

Whenever Zahra Jan came here, Mother gave me a dirty look. She used to say that Zahra Jan was a pilferer. She told me that, as the saying goes, someone who steals eggs will steal a camel. She said that if a sapling doesn't grow straight, it will stay forever bent. Mother said a lot more. I didn't listen to her, though. Zahra Jan was chatty and cheerful. She knew how to keep mother's cloud from raining on her parade. Mother said, "This girl's as cheerful and sunny as you're bad-tempered and grumpy." It's true I was cranky, but I enjoyed my time with Zahra Jan. She was three or four years older. She didn't go to school; she climbed up trees and walls as much as she could. Other than me, she played most of her time with neighbourhood boys. Really naughty, she was their leader. When Mother wasn't home, Zahra Jan collected worms from the flowerbed and snails from the hollow where water collected by the pool and frightened the neighbourhood girls with them. She didn't frighten me. She taught me how to hunt cockroaches, how to set a trap for sparrows, how to pull off the cats' whiskers. She carried me on her shoulders and ran around the pool. She took dolls, marbles, whirligigs, and a yo-yo from me. If she wanted something that I wouldn't give her, she'd scowl but wouldn't argue, though her home didn't have what she wanted.

At the end of the yard, we'd tied ropes to the ash-tree to make a swing. We went there and swung. She could sit and leap for the rope over and over. She swung with the wind up to the top of their house's wall. Watching her made me feel dizzy. My heart beat fast until she came back to earth. Her two plaits shot straight in the air like two horns at the back of her head. The wind puffed under her skirt and her pants became puffy too. The heels of her big feet, which were always bare, were cracked and crusted. There was always soil between her fingers and under her long nails. When the swing slowed down, she started to spin with it; she spun and laughed. When it was my turn, she got off. She cautiously sat me down on the ropes. She slowly pushed my back so that I could swing. The sun poured into my eyes from between the leaves. I closed my eyes. The wind whistled by my ears. She gradually pushed me harder. I was scared; at the same time, I enjoyed it. When it was cloudy, riding on the swing, we seemed to reach the lanes of clouds. The scent of orange flowers made us drunk. One day Zahra Jan said, "These orange flowers are mine." I said, "No." She became upset. She said she wouldn't let me attend her wedding. "You can have all the orange flowers."

The day that Zahra Jan became a bride, I was upset because I couldn't blow bubble-gum. I stretched the tip of my tongue to make the gum extra-thin. I blew into it but couldn't make a balloon. So, I could do it,

Zahra Jan took my gum and chewed it. She blew rapidly and successively and exploded it with a pop. The big and small balloons, yellow and blue and pink, constantly appeared and disappeared from her bud-like lips.

The day there had been a wedding party in the house of our next-door neighbour, Narges Banu, the orange tree was young and slender. Among its shiny green locks of hair were clusters of milky flowers, lots of stars, stars that would become suns. Then my tree would become full of suns. At the time I didn't know that.

Narges Banu knew that. She sat beside the oven. Drops of sweat appeared on her olive face. She reddened from the heat. Her cheeks became rosy. Her eyes narrowed. Zahra Jan was ten years old. Narges Banu was still young. Her plaits were jet black and long, like lassos. She baked bread at home and had Zahra Jan deliver it to houses for sale. But I used to go straight to her oven and get fresh hot bread. Narges Banu made *nasiri*, crisped rice, too. Zahra Jan arranged them in a tray, and roamed around the lanes to sell them. Whenever I went to their home, Narges Banu put a ball of *Nasiri*, rice cake, in my hand. She didn't accept payment. Whenever Zahra Jan was home, we played together. When she was not home, I stayed around for a while. I sat on the edge of the veranda in front of their room and watched Narges

Banu. She kneaded soft white dough with her big coarse brown hands and rapidly made cakes of it. Her eyelashes were white from flour dust. Her thin lips made a bud. She hummed a song. As long as she was busy with the dough, she didn't feel like talking. When she went to the oven, she began to talk non-stop. When she complained how naughty Zahra Jan caused problems, the thin crescents of her eyebrows joined. When she lamented about her loneliness and how forlorn she was, the nostrils of her big bony nose shivered. When she told about hard times, she smiled bitterly. When she related tales of Zahra Jan's father, her eyes filled with anger. When she talked about her village, her voice became soft.

Narges Banu knew that the tree would be filled with oranges. Smilingly, she asked me to pick them for her. Her teeth were big and white. I said no. She didn't ask me why. She didn't know that those orange flowers of spring would belong to Zahra Jan.

Now it's autumn. The wind has turned the thin layers of far grey clouds into threads. In the midst of the sky, the inner folds of the cottony clouds have become as thin as glass. They look as bright and transparent as water – like azure silk. But if it rains, maybe Zahra Jan won't come.

I go to the corner of the veranda. I look over the wall at their house. It's abandoned. In a corner there's a well that's been covered in recent years. In the other corner there's an empty hen house with a black open mouth. In the centre of the courtyard there's a small muddy pool and, here and there around the pool, weeds and thick shrubs. The oven set into the middle of the veranda has been cold for a long time. In the joins of the dark brown earthen bricks and among the rotten termite-eaten timbers of the roof are dry straw-coloured weeds. Here and there are piles of trash. The rusty locks of the rooms' wooden doors show that she hasn't come yet. The windows stare at me with dull, cracked, glassy eyes. When the tree had its first spring of flowering, Zahra Jan became a bride. The second flowering spring Zahra Jan, Narges Banu, and her son-in-law moved away from the house next to ours. And now Zahra Jan is coming back to witness the eighth year of the tree's flowering in the company of her little sister.

I saw Zahra Jan on my way back home from school. From morning to the afternoon, it had rained, but the sky was still cloudy. Passing by the shabby houses around the railroad, noisily splashing, I strolled along the muddy path in my black plastic boots. The air after the rain made me feel heavy and damp. I saw Zahra Jan in the door of a hut. She was gazing into the middle distance, as if waiting for somebody or something. She was dressed in black. Her bare feet were in loose rubber boots. The tips of her twin henna-coloured plaits stuck out of her big headscarf. She carried Abji tucked up in a faded chador. Abji's blonde forelock of her bent, sleeping head was visible from behind Zahra Jan's slim arm.

I didn't want to see Zahra Jan. I'd thought that she wouldn't be home then. I knew that she had started to work in the factory after Narges Banu quit working. I knew that when Zahra Jan became a widow, Narges Banu went insane. I knew that when Zahra Jan became a bride, Narges Banu became pregnant. I knew that.... No, I didn't want to know. When I took a short-cut home and passed by the huts after they'd moved from our neighbourhood, I sometimes saw Zahra Jan. We didn't talk much. I didn't want to get home late and she didn't want to be late for work. She said that she missed her old house. She wished they could go back to it. When Azizollah, Zahra Jan's husband, was alive, she talked about him. She said that he was cranky and glowering and sometimes frightened her. I didn't ask her anything. She told me whatever she wanted. Words came out from her lips slow and disconnected. While talking, her eyes looked restless and frightened. Her bony nose looked sharper. Her skin looked yellowish.

Her mouth sloped, as if with each word she was losing part of her life.

Azizollah was a baker. Sometimes, when I went to buy bread, I saw him. I was afraid of him and didn't go near him. I thought he must have been dreadful if Zahra Jan had been afraid of him. He was young and tall and thin. He had a thin drooping moustache, big bluish protruding lips, and small black eyes. The deep black of his eyes dazzled me. I got scared. I averted my eyes from his face and eyes. I stared at his apron stained with dough. The red, purple, orange, and yellow flames from the oven played across his long horsy profile. They reminded me of a dragon and also of Zahra Jan, who'd once been so bold.

After Abji was born, Zahra Jan started to talk about her. She was always tied to Zahra Jan's back. When Zahra Jan looked at the baby, her eyes shone — in the past her eyes had shone too when she looked at my cotton doll. She didn't pay attention to people's sarcasm. People said that Abji was illegitimate; Zahra Jan smiled and shrugged. People said that she was paralyzed because she was a bastard. Zahra Jan's eyes grew tearful, a frown appeared on her forehead, and her face wrinkled in anger. With a lump in her throat, she started swearing and cursing and pulling at her hair. When Azizollah died in a fire, she neither wept nor pulled out her hair. People said that his death was divine punishment. But she said that it was Abji who looked like him. She said that she wanted to work hard and save money to take the baby to Tehran to be cured. Unlike her, Narges Banu could not stand the baby and the new misery.

Zahra Jan said that Narges Banu roamed through the lanes and gathered children around her. Snapping her fingers, she sang for them. She danced sometimes and wept other times. Once in a while she got a can of gas and matches and when she had children and other passers-by around her she'd say she'd set fire to herself. When people believed her, she'd throw the can of gas and matches away and, in between weeping and laughter, she'd start to sing.

The last time I had seen Narges Banu she wasn't insane. It was sunset and it rained. The air was laden with the scent of spring flowers. I was standing in the shelter of our house's front door. Azizollah had brought a cart and taken their furniture. Zahra Jan had left with the cart. Apparently, Narges Banu didn't like to leave her house, or maybe she wanted to leave the house when it was dark and quiet. A heavy cover of rain clouds filled the space between the dark sky and the muddy ground of the lane — packed rows of diagonal fine-woven grey curtains. The gutters sang. The soft breeze and cold rain touched my cheeks and palms and passed. When I was about to go inside, I saw Narges Banu. This time, uncharacteristically, she wore her chador tight around her face. She looked around anxiously. I said hello to her. She barely nodded. She looked worried and embarrassed. A wan smile appeared on her lips. Her eyes were full of sorrow and tears. Her lips moved slightly. She turned and hastily left.

When Zahra Jan saw me, she pulled my arm, inviting me in. I said I didn't want to be home late. In fact, I didn't want to see Narges Banu. She suggested we go to the railroad track. I didn't ask why. I followed her. With the pace of Zahra Jan's steps, the big head and chubby bare legs of Abji gently swung. The rails were wet and shinny, like the big and little pebbles around them. In the distance, on top of the dark green hill, the Safi Aabad monument, with its rows of sharp-pointed cypress, thrust its head into the thick dark blue mist. We stood beside the railroad. A black patch of cloud hovered over our heads. Abji, woken up, was staring at me in surprise. Her eyes were small and black. Her cheeks had the same colour as the pink sweetbriars of the Bagh-e Shah monument. She smiled. Zahra Jan turned to me. Abji's smile was hidden behind Zahra Jan's shoulder. The white of Zahra Jan's eyes looked greyish. She had a blank look. She tightly pursed her lips.

A small mole on her chin was like a seed of wild rue. I wanted to say something. We heard the whistle of the train in distance. Startled, she slipped on the pebbles. She righted herself and stared at me. Her eyes were full of fear. Her skin looked bruised. Wrinkles appeared in the corners of her lips. "It was here," she said hoarsely. Her chin quivered. The train's roar became louder. Frightened, she pulled me aside. Her hand was cold and wet. Without looking at me, she said brokenly, "My Mom threw her under the train here, did you know that?" The black dragon roared. It sent out smoke from its chest and crawled on iron feet. I couldn't breathe for a moment. There was a light in the sky and then the thunder burst. Abji cried and bumped her head against Zahra Jan's shoulder blade. Zahra Jan and I started to run in the shower.

I sit on the edge of the veranda and pick up a leaf from a branch of the tree. The two parts of the leaf are attached at the bottom, one big, the other small. The small part reminds me of Abji who has always been stuck to Zahra Jan's back. It is fall and I'm waiting. When Zahra Jan comes, every orange flower of spring will be hers.

# WAXINA

I wish you weren't so hard! But don't think that I'm upset with you, too – no way! That I'm noisily chewing gum and tapping you non-stop, click, click, clicking isn't because I'm mad at the guy here. He thinks he can upset me. Thank God I'm so good-natured that I never get upset. If I bug him, it's not my fault. It's not my fault that the boss put both of us in one room because he claims there's a space shortage. You know why he did it. He wishes to hear me complaining about the lack of space or this typing job so that he can grin and slip his glasses down his plump nose with the tip of his thick finger and stare at me over his glasses with those ox-eyes of his and soften his deep voice and say, "I've advised you many times to stop being a typist. Being a secretary would be more suitable ..." Well, the poor man can't help it. He assumes that I'm an 18-year-old girl. Now, if you could speak, you'd surely say, "Come on, he knows perfectly well that you're a divorced mature woman." But you can't speak for yourself, right? You can't say you're my punching bag, doomed to take everything I say until you explode. No, I'm not a perpetual complainer. Well, I don't have any problems, and I'm not one to exaggerate. But maybe I'm a little bit mouthy. Maybe I was born like that. All I need is ears to hear me. Where can I find ears though? As my Granny says, I've got a talent for making friends easily, but from early morning till late afternoon I sit down here and type page after page. Well, you can't become friends with men because they get you wrong. With women it isn't easier: if they're married, they're wary, if not, they're not mature enough. All of them, male or female, young or old, are the same. Whoever you approach, you see a big-mouthed egomaniac. Now you may say I'm the same too. Well, maybe you're right. But I'm not enough of a dummy to open my big mouth in front of dummies. That my chewing bugs my co-worker is another story. If he hadn't been so crabby, he'd be married by now. He badmouths the boss and everybody else, not just me. He's not a bad-looking guy but something's wrong with him. Maybe he's one of those crazy Commies who want to kick out the Shah. I don't know, he's different. The way he frowns and puffs his cigarette and chews the tip of his moustache.... Maybe he's just short-tempered and the sound of a click is enough to get up his nose. If that's the case, it's his problem. When he fills the office with smoke, or slams the door, or frowns for no reason, I don't get upset. If he complains to the boss, I'll be rid of him. Yet he doesn't do that. He knows that the boss is coming on to me. Surely, he also knows that I don't pay attention to the boss or any other guy. I'm not hostile, though. I don't care what they have in their empty heads. I shouldn't do anything naughty — well, I don't. But it's ridiculous not to chew my gum in order to keep my honour safe and sound! He thinks like my Granny, who used to say, "Sweetheart, a good decent girl never chews gum." My poor Granny keeps her mouth shut now. Well, what can she say, when she's half-deaf? Ever since I came back with my suitcase in one hand and my baby in the other, she stopped saying do this and don't do that. It's been so long that when she remembers what happened, she begins to cry and slap her head. I keep telling her, "Well, dearest Granny, how could you know what would happen to me? It was just my fate..." But that doesn't calm her down. I say, "Believe me, Granny, I'm OK. I make a living by myself and can support my child. I don't need a man to support me..." Yet these words don't relieve her. She thinks that she caused me misery. She kept insisting. I said, "Granny, please..." But she insisted, "I do my motherly duty. Your macho father married right after your mother died young and now he thinks that he's doing me a favour by paying me a monthly allowance." I said, "But you're making me marry a photo." She said, "Well, I got his photo so that you see that he isn't old and ugly. In my time, there was no photo." Now, she's put the same photo in a frame and propped it on the mantelpiece and doesn't let me take it away. Why? So my child at least knows what her father looks like. I don't want her to know that at all! But I'm not stubborn. If this makes the old woman happy, let it be. My little daughter stands in front of the mantelpiece and stares at the photo whenever she feels blue. Maybe my poor baby soothes herself this way. I don't know. Don't think this angers or upsets me. Not at all! I'm not angry, by any means, either with the guy whose sperm gave me life, or with that useless drug addict who never thought why other people shouldn't be his slaves, or with this boss who keeps coming on to me, or even with this thick-moustached fella who can't stand my chewing gum and the click, click, click of my typewriter. Well, that's why I'm always cheerful. At most he could say that I'm trivial, or that my breath stinks – whatever, I don't care. Or the other guy, he might dream up a new technique to get me – but I'm sick of changing my job and going from this company to that company, when you get the same story anywhere. On top of that, who says that my co-worker doesn't have intentions of his own? Maybe if he had a chance he'd do what others would do — well, you never know. But despite all these worries, I won't give up. There's no doubt that I'm safe and sound and my kid is with me and that makes me thankful. That I yack too much is because I'm cheerful. Certainly, you don't feel like chatting when you're blue. You know what? I'm like the girl in the story Granny told a hundred or a thousand times. They made her marry a young handsome merchant and she thought that she was really lucky. Then one day the merchant says that he has to start travelling a lot and the girl should always stay home alone and not socialize with anybody. So the girl gets upset, wondering what to do in that big house. She opens the doors of the rooms one by one. One room is full of fabrics, the other is full of jewels, and the other full of wax, etc. But what's the use of these rooms full of stuff when she doesn't have company? All the doors are locked, but there's a way up to the roof. I got out myself that way. But that girl is very smart and, as Granny used to say, she's a good decent girl. So, she makes Waxina lest loneliness tempt her into sin. It was this silent Waxina who eventually leads the girl to happiness and Granny's story had a happy ending. Oh, why are my fingertips pins and needles? What if you were soft and yielding? Now if you ask me how I know that Waxina was soft and yielding, I say that I don't know. But the girl was surely young and nice and made Waxina the same way. Well, we all like to have folks who are exactly like us – that's for sure. I have to confess that as my little daughter grows up sometimes, I think about how much she resembles me. By the way, I shouldn't forget to buy her a doll at the end of the month. She wants to have one of these tall slim Barbies. Well, if I buy her a doll, I can't afford perfume for myself. She has priority, though. She doesn't see me from morning to night. I can barely take her to a movie or a park on weekends. Also she doesn't have any playmates. She's always home with Granny. She should have dolls and toys to play with. I can wait. Don't you think so? I think I'm doomed to be content with my little daughter's company. After all, she's my own flesh and blood. Granny won't be with us much longer and then the kid won't have anybody but me, and I won't have anybody but her. I've got no complains, but sometimes I do wonder. Why on earth should an easy-going outgoing person like me lack company in such a big world full of different people? I might have been ready to get along with the poor guy if he'd given me any hope. Well, now I think so, but at that time I thought different. During the six months he quit drugs, he didn't make life easier for me. I should have finished right off the bat. But I was naïve and sympathized with his mother and her woes. I thought that it might go well eventually. But it didn't, and on top of that, a baby landed in my lap. It was the time he temporarily quit that I realized I was afraid of him, not anything else, just him. He wasn't horrible-looking.

Nothing was wrong with how he looked. But when he gazed at me with his fish-eyes, my whole body froze. I hated him, myself, the world. He didn't have a heart, not just for me but even for his mother. His mother used to say that he hadn't been like that before. I didn't believe it though. He didn't see me at all, not only me, but others. He was just concerned about himself. His mother, maybe to try to make me stay, used to say that men were all like that. She said that we women should just get along with them, somehow take care of them. Well, maybe that was what that poor woman did all her life so she expected me to do the same. When he pulled the gold good-luck necklace off the baby's neck, I said to myself that enough was enough. But don't think that I hate him! I feel sorry for him. What happened to me happened many years ago just like you might talk about some poor guy, and I'd feel sympathy for him. I'm no vengeful camel. If I'd been vengeful, I wouldn't have donated money to charity every Thursday so that God would bless a father who never did anything nice to me, or I wouldn't have taken care of Granny, who sealed my fate with an arranged marriage. Now poor Granny's in bed all day, waiting for me to come back from work and help her. Well, it's time to leave for the day. I gotta go. The fridge is empty. It takes time to do shopping, and I won't get home till after dark. Thank God the boss was busy enough not to bother me today. Or, maybe, my co-worker has bitched about me, since he hasn't come back yet. But his briefcase is still here, next to his chair. Does he dislike me that much that he won't pick up his briefcase till after I'm gone? Well, it's true that I'd like to be still clicking away when he opens the door and comes in. I've also kept this old chewing gum in my mouth for the same reason. But don't imagine that I'm waiting around for him! I wonder, though, why he doesn't like me. If I had been ugly, then my boss wouldn't have tried so hard to come on to me. Damn it! Sometimes I'm tempted to give him a green light just to bug my co-worker. But I can't stand what he looks like. Now if Granny knows what I have in mind, she'll blame me. Still, I don't dare to chew gum around her. Although she doesn't criticize me anymore, the way she looks at me makes me lose my confidence. Not that I'm afraid of her, but I respect her. I owe her a lot. Maybe that's why she used to dictate to me. Sure, she had good intentions and wished me well. Even when she pinched me, she did it for my own good. That's what she's said many, many times. She hasn't had anybody else in the world other than me after her daughter died young. God knows how many times I've swallowed what was on the tip of my tongue. But maybe it wasn't all kindness and consideration. Who knows, maybe one day I'll speak up and complain about how she pinched me hard on the last night of each month when my lousy father turned up. Well, she vented her anger on me because she couldn't fight him. No doubt a motherless kid is always a burden no matter where she is. That was why I couldn't leave my innocent baby with my mother-in-law. She couldn't have been better than my Granny... Or maybe she could have been. Although Granny seemed to be good-natured, she was a tyrant too. Even now she indirectly runs the house. I make a living, and I pay the bills, but she's the boss. Sweetheart, that's not the right place for the turmeric! Honey, one shouldn't stay over so late! My dear, it's not good for a young woman to be out at night! Sweetie, there is a right way to raise a baby girl.... Shit! Once there was no end to her grumbles, now there is no end to her advice! I'm fed up with her. Well, I'm tired. What can I do? It's good that you don't have eyes to give me a dirty look. Instead, I ignore the fact that you don't have a tongue. Waxina, who that girl made in the shape and size of a human being, wasn't that different from you. Of course, she was soft and good-looking, yet like you she didn't see or say anything. To tell the truth, I know that here's not the right place for me. You don't open your mouth and that guy doesn't open his eyes to see me. Certainly, Granny doesn't make me hopeful. So, the only one left is that kid who, now, I bet, is crouching in a corner of the old woman's room, staring at the door and waiting for me and ... then ... no, well, how I can say it? I know that it's late. I don't want to see that guy anymore, let alone want him to soften his heart. Not only I don't want to see him, but I don't want to see anybody. That's because I'm down-hearted and deeply depressed. Well, how long should I keep my mouth shut and angrily chew my gum? How long should I not say a word to an acquaintance or a stranger or even to my picture in the mirror and even to myself, lest paradise, the promised place for mothers, shakes under my feet? Well, you poor thing, it makes sense that you don't know anything about softness. I cram my words one by one into your head; you're a dummy and a dolt. So, you can't blame me for not getting up ... Well, what the hell will happen if it gets so dark that I can't find the way to my damned house? What else? Hmmm, I haven't said my last word? Well, even if I don't say that to myself, I say it to you because you don't have eyes, or ears, or tongue. Then I'll leave you alone, I'll pack up, I'll swallow my old chewing gum and I'll leave quietly the way I always do. I'll shop and I'll arrive home with hands full of shopping bags. Turning the key in the keyhole, I'll tell the Devil to go to hell. I'll open the door with a big smile. But when I'm at the door to my room, I'll freeze. I'll hate myself, and the world, and ... and this kid. Yes, I hate my own kid, my own daughter... for she gazes at me with fish eyes .... Well, OK, I don't say anything anymore, and I don't want anything anymore, but how is it that I can swallow all these hard things at the same time as you get hard and harder to my touch?

# KHODADAD IS HAPPY

The door does not lead out, and the window, a mat draped across it, does not admit anything except noise and dust. I am falling down the well of my room, my cave, my crypt. I close my eyes. What the eyes evade the ears pick up. The crash of picks and axes coming from the house next door, the short croak of a lone crow, the squeal of a motorbike turning at the lane's dead end, the long howl of the abandoned puppy in a corner of the desolate vacant lot, the groan and moan of a second-hand dealer's old pick-up truck, the rat-a-tat of a woman's heels, the crackle and scuff of a child's slippers on the sidewalk. All these mixed minor repetitive sounds are nothing next to the laughter I hear.

*In the beginning was the Laughter, and the Laughter was with Khodadad, and the Laughter was Khodadad.* It seems to me that only a little further, beyond a curtain not always apparent, sadness lies in quiet dreadful ambush. Does this mat hung across my window secure my realm at night? The distance between Khodadad's exhausted body lying on a worn-out bed and this room's loneliness is no more than a few spans. No light comes from behind my closed eyelids.

The disturbed mind pushes sleep back. To entertain myself, I intertwine the bantering, sarcastic voices of men I hear outside, piecing them together in a word-woven quilt:

"This family isn't the first or last."

"You said it. This guy, Morteza Akhavan, he knew how to do it. His old man, Mojtaba, God bless him, he worked hard all his life, but he still couldn't support his family. Morteza was just a kid when the Revolution hit. But he was smart enough to push his father into grabbing a building when the owner fled the country."

"And now he isn't alive to see his son asking for 400,000 tomans a square metre."

"Damn it! The construction's a drag for all of us. They offload bricks and beams at midnight, piles of earth and stone – the worst is the welding workshop in the middle of our lane!"

"Well, you know why the regime's poverty-stricken supporters..."

"Sure, thanks to God and the municipal zoners, the houses they grab from the filthy rich become nice brand-new low-rise rental buildings with elevators and open-plan kitchens..."

"Fuck it! A rental building on such a tiny site!"

"Well, nothing matters except bribing the city councillors..."

"That's why if we file a complaint it won't work."

"Meanwhile the guy renting flats is busy volunteering with the community mosque, the community committee, the community cooperative...."

"Every morning you see a new high rise building pop up in your face. The regime's fans think the whole country belongs to them. And you don't expect them to take advantage!"

"Well, you can't cry, 'O Absent Saint, show your face and right the wrongs of the world! Make it snappy!' Unless there's trouble! Hey, Khodadad, what do you think? Didn't you escape from the evil Taliban in Afghanistan and take refuge in nice safe Iran?"

I push back my word-woven quilt. The echo of Khodadad's laughter tightens a necklace around my neck. Now and then, I heard this strange sound behind a wall or window. His exotic accent and soft tones, his dry cough and wheezy voice, his narrow eyes and lame leg, his skinny body, half covered in dust. All these, are nothing but redundancy on the margin of his flag of laughter, marks the margin of my days.

In the dark of the cave, I am crushed by debris from a continuous collapse. A horde of Afghans have invaded, axes, picks, and shovels over their shoulders. The attack's uproar fills the swarming lanes and lanes; new buildings remorselessly mushroom, a windfall for the rich winners and the minimum-wage losers.

The night's immune from laughter. Khodadad, the Afghan, fails to see profits even in his dreams. However, as long as the dust he inhales offers him a place to sleep he can burst out laughing, relieved to have a job. Khodadad is happy without a permanent roof over his head, without a mate or a friend. But behind this drape and within this refuge I have remained day and night so heavy and dull that the gap between his laughter and my weariness seems insurmountable.

From time to time I hear crickets chirp. I remember the flight back to Iran and the transit lounge in Rome, and Leonardo, the handsome airport employee who smiles and laughs through our discomfort. A fellow passenger complains, "We're in transit. Before our flight we have to stay here for three days and two nights. It's so cold at night we can't sleep without blankets. If you can't keep us warm what the hell are you doing?"

Answering in broken English, Leonardo assures us that he understands. If we want a nice warm, cosy, comfortable place to stay, we – the women, anyway – can go home with him. Pleasant, smiling, he makes sure we get the message before he says a word in Italian and leaves us alone.

We wander around the big, bright, noisy transit lounge. Lingering in front of shop windows, we change the prices in lira and U.S. dollars to tomans; envious, we turn our back to the windows. Several times counting the dollars that remain, we cautiously order a small sandwich and a glass of orange juice, glad that we are able to bring back a few dollar bills as souvenirs for our families at the price of eating little, avoiding shopping, and disregarding our strong desire to visit the magnificent city. Irrationally afraid of AIDS, we go to the washroom reluctantly but obsessively, washing our faces and secretly taking off our head scarves, the mark of our country, from our head and hair, in the meantime watching blondes elaborately make themselves up; milling around. Downstairs, we run into a crowd of Asian, African, and Bosnian refugees under arrest, indigent and helpless, waiting and crumpling, exhausted from their heavy hand luggage, backpacks, and fruitless wanderings. We take benches to nap or watch people around us — the endless comings and goings and sittings and standings; the vertiginous parade of passengers; the variety of fashion and models; the mix of interwoven languages and voices; the sparrow-like horde of affluent polite Japanese; the facial makeup of elderly American ladies in tourist groups; the slovenliness of a group of dark, black-eyed women and children; the carelessness of the airport staff answering passengers' questions; the genuflection and prostration of an old Iranian woman wrapped in her veil and preoccupied with prayer in the middle of the lounge — on her way for a visit to her son, who runs a nightclub in L.A. — and the grins of Leonardo as he goes by.

Vainly I keep closing my eyes. Leonardo's smile vanishes in the dullness of my crypt. I collapse voicelessly. In distressful dreams, Leonardo da Vinci Airport becomes a disastrous night of losers. I stare at them, confused: the silent demonstration of outcast refugees — exhausted bodies, lean faces, eyes full of horror. Going back and forth, they topple over me, penetrate into, settle down within me and remain forever. I have seen these aliens in the far or near light and shade of the present and of history. Asad, the Sudanese, does not know Leo Africanus; Zlata of Bosnia does not expect the happy ending of her Sarajevo namesake's *Zlata's Diary*. Recalling the victorious invasions of the famous Saladin does not cure the blistered body of Soleiman of Kurdistan. The nightmare of the Mehran and Multan refugee camps in Pakistan has branded the mind of Nizar, the Iraqi. Iqbal Banu, the Pakistani, has nothing to do with the famous singer of the same name. Bakhtiar, the Iranian, midway to a free country, almost dead after what happened to him in Bucharest, does not remember Dr. Shapur Bakhtiar, the Iranian politician murdered in Paris. No one puts a candle in the palm of their stretched hands, nor does Leonardo cajole them into a smile.

I do not see a way out. The night, along with the chirp of crickets, has ended. Zaynab, the daughter of the First Imam, is alone in the desert of Karbala after her brother's army has been slaughtered. The soil of a wasteland does not let anything familiar appear. I open my eyes. The morning light passes across my well=s opening. The day is emptied of the laughter of Khodadad that had stuffed the void. Won't I hear his laughter anymore? A prey to Taliban or a morsel in the mouth of a grave... Whichever, the exotic sound has vanished forever, as if there has never ever been the Laughter at the beginning or before the beginning of space and time. Or, if it has been there, it has not existed with Khodadad, or Khodadad has never existed; and... Whatever there is and whatever there is not, weariness has lain somewhere in ambush. My room, my cave, my crypt becomes my grave.

# OF MUTTS AND MEN

## I

It was the sound that severed me from the nightmare --
the new sound, the little sound. The light behind the
frosted glass is now dim. The opening eyes have been
wounded by light. The sound of the abandoned puppy!
How soon his mother left him alone! I've seen the bitch
two or three times in the early morning or early evening.
Cautious during the day, she keeps her distance — no
sight or sound from her. Yet she's nervous: wanders the
vacant lot, hides behind a tree, takes refuge beyond a
wall. A helpless sound. Did Yusef call me from the
bottom of the well? The hand stretched vainly in the air
drops. The puppy, ignorant of the bitch's worries,
wanders confused along the edge of the lane. Will he
survive?

I linger beside his room's door. I lean my hand
against the door frame — my legs are weak. Did the
sound come from beyond that room's window or from
beyond this door? From wherever it was, the sound
called me. If I have no answer, no solutions, I must be
silent. The house's front door opens.

"Don't forget your promise, Dad," Yusef calls out.

"No, I won't. I'll buy you toys today like every day. Bye."

That's it. The door closes. So he has been awake, but he hasn't called me. Why did I fall asleep? Am I as careless as a bitch? I didn't hear the shot. Or did I? I open his door. I put on the mask of a morning smile. The pale light has dulled his pale complexion. I haven't been checkmated yet. Have I? Old voices come to me again:

"Be careful, you shouldn't get checked so much and so soon!"

"But I haven't been checkmated yet."

"You haven't? But one of these checks will be checkmate."

Constant checks! The sword hovering over my head moves only a little — not to fall but just to remind me. His flat forehead is sweaty.

"Why didn't you wake me up?" I ask.

A turtle dove has perched on the windowsill of his room.

"Do you have pain again?" I ask.

The turtle dove moves.

"Are you feeling hot?" I ask.

The turtle dove flies away. He frowns.

"Would you like me to open the window?" I ask.

Turning his head away, he says, bored, impatient, "Gosh, you ask so many questions, Mom?"

I go to the kitchen. I make his breakfast. While I'm putting the tray on the bedside table, he asks, "How long should I stay in bed?"

"Until you get well."

"What if I don't get well?"

I don't answer him.

"Huh?"

My smiling mask is still in place.

"If Granny was here, she'd say, 'Bite your tongue and don't be a naysayer!' She's coming to stay with you today."

I wipe the sweat off his forehead with a paper tissue.

"So today you're going to the office. Do you have to go?" he says.

"My leave is over. I'll take more if I have to, though."

Giving me his half-empty cup of tea, he says, "You mean if I don't get well."

I open the window. "Be patient!" I say gently.

"Until when?" he asks short-temperedly.

"Until the doctors find out why your legs hurts."

Clenching his hands into fists, he says, "I will not go to the hospital or to the lab again."

"You mean you don't want to get up and walk again!"

"When I put my feet on the ground, they hurt a lot. I'm the one who's hurting, not you."

Don't I suffer? Granny comes. Climbing the stairs has made her out of breath. She rubs her palms on her painful knees. I offer her a cup of tea.

"I've come here so that you can go to work. Just tell me what his medication is!" she says.

In the high-buttoned manteau I must wear to work, I say, "For the time being he doesn't have any drugs. He doesn't have a fever anymore. If he's in pain he can take a pain killer. He knows which one. And for lunch..."

"For lunch I know what to do. You can go."

I take my purse. I kiss Yusef's damp hair. "Call me if you have to!" I say.

He's watching the turtle dove perching on a branch of the tree outside the window.

"Did you hear what I said?"

He turns to me. "Don't make her fly away again," he whispers.

I leave the room quietly. While I'm opening the front door, I hear Granny calling me, "When did he come back?"

"Who?" I ask, confused.

She means the Shah. Once again, I forgot the compulsory veil. "So once again she's forgotten to wear her headscarf. Is that right, Granny?" Yusef says loudly.

So again, the turtle dove has flown away. I yank the black headscarf from the clothes hanger.

## II

The long lane and above it the cloudy ceiling; the grass has started to show in the border of the vacant lot, though. Neither the bitch nor her puppy is in sight. Behind the stacks of bricks, boys wait in ambush — but with empty hands, no stone or stick or sling. They stare at me until I disappear around the corner. Cats and crows prowl around the piles of garbage bags. "*Our city, our home*" — that's the city's current slogan. What slogan has made a dog *mofsed-e fel-arz*, a corruptor of society? Last night I didn't hear the shot. Did I? Not always, but once in a while you hear nothing but barking in the lane, shattering the night. Eventually somebody dials the telephone number and at dawn you also hear the dogcatcher's truck. The wheels stop. The click of the trigger, and the sound of the shot and ... then ... a howl and a moan. So is it over? You exhale. You open your eyes. You see the signs of morning on the window's frosted glass. You close your eyes again. You push your face against the pillow and try to smother the image of the puppy, unaware that barking dogs must be destroyed. Don't you hear the new voice? I hear the old voices:

"Old dogs go, but a puppy always survives."

"But not to live long, just long enough to produce more puppies."

"Maybe it's a manifestation of Satyagraha."

"Passive resistance? The bitch doesn't turn down the chance to make more puppies and ignore fate."

"But Adam eats the forbidden fruit and accepts fate."

"Punishment is primary, not sin. Punishment is a kind of fate. The gates of the hell in which Raskolnikov is burning will not open with murdering the old woman."

"So maybe sin sometimes guides us to purgatory ..."

"That night when the woman left home to go out, was it moonlit?"

The night scene is all I can recall from Pearl Buck's story "The Mother." I don't remember now if the woman in it thought what she did was a sin or not.

"...And the old woman. Wouldn't she see Raskolnikov as her saviour if she had a life like Job, or if she was supposed to have that kind of life?"

"But if Raskolnikov commits a major sin and in search of salvation chooses definite suffering rather than the distress of confusion, the Chinese mother, upset about unjustified punishment, takes refuge in sin."

"When punishment is the decisive justification, being innocent equals being guilty. Joseph K. must be put on trial, and the trial, per se, means punishment. That's it."

"So, in the beginning was the punishment and... later was the sin that ..."

Disturbing daydream and the long lane and the gloomy day. Why don't I hear the sound of spring when my Yusef can still be cheered up by a small timid turtle dove?

At the bus stop I sit on the bench next to a bulky woman covered in a black *chador*. I pull my black headscarf forward. Something plops heavily on my headscarf. I look up. Above me a crow, standing over a hole in the roof of the open-sided bus shelter, doesn't budge. I look down. I pull out a crumpled paper tissue from the pocket of my black manteau. The woman wrapped in black chador watches me with her mouth open. I turn my face away. Granny always says, "Whatever God does is with wisdom, even his wrath or anger ..." The old voices echo:

"So there is wisdom in everything, including objects ... for instance, in Pahlavi brief shorts..."

"But why are the shorts called Pahlavi?"

"There must be a wisdom in that, too. Apparently before the Pahlavi dynasty the Qajars used to cover their private parts with sort of loose pants ... So snug-fitting Pahlavi shorts were a form of progress ..."

"The poor woman is upset. No wonder she forgets to wear a headscarf when, from early morning on, she has to do all her housework and supervise her kids' homework and think about buying and selling and trading ration coupons and how long and wide the queues are going to be!"

"The woman next door tells her they're distributing cooking oil at a subsidized price. She thinks that if she doesn't rush, she won't get it. So she hurries and holds her toddler in her arms and rushes to the co-op store, with no headscarf on her head."

"You know what? The lane was quiet and if one or two passersby happened to pass, they didn't feel like guiding her at that hour. For sure her toddler, just starting to talk, couldn't help."

"At the entrance to the bazaar, when she sees the Morality Squad police and people try to warn her with gestures, she notices ..."

"Her shopping bag was plastic, not cloth."

"She digs into her bag, looking for her kid's Pahlavi shorts..."

"No way! She takes them off the toddler."

"She's got no choice other than cover her head with the shorts."

"Oh, yeah, later when she's out of danger from the Morality Squad and the tragic story turns comic, she realizes the benefit of those kind of shorts."

"But if the shorts weren't Pahlavi shorts and had two legs, wouldn't the police have arrested her?"

"The Pahlavi shorts could keep danger away, so they were useful, but what was the point of a big can of gasoline and matches with them a woman set herself on fire on the street to protest the compulsory veil?"

"Clearly it was a relief to the woman who protested by doing that. And it made hot news."

"My goodness! Even when you're not allowed to speak you won't stop speaking out!"

The bulky woman wrapped in the black chador gets up and shakes the dust off it. The bus approaches.

The crow hasn't moved. A cat, who'd got his morning ration from the nearby butcher's, strolls along the sidewalk and leaps up onto the bench. I get up. The bus stops — men enter from the front door, women from the middle door. The woman grabs the handrail and goes to the left. The women's section is crowded. I go to the right. No women's seats are available, but all the men get one. Several teen-age girls with maqna'ehs (full head covers) enclosing their faces and a woman with a baby in her arms climb on board behind me. The bus moves. The crow croaks and leaps down beside the cat, who's lounging in a corner of the bench -- peaceful co-existence. Did cats and crows propose the bill in the Parliament to kill stray dogs? Using the edges of their maqna'ehs as shields, the girls murmur and giggle. The woman with a baby, who also holds a heavy sack in her hand and staggers with every lurch of the bus, responds to her baby's distress with a grumble. At the next stop a man in the last row of seats gets off. The woman gratefully drops into the free spot. The man sitting next to her gives her a sideways glance and draws himself away. "Poor guy, his territory's been invaded," mumbles one of the girls, who is clutching a binder and a few books. Her bangs are jet-black and she has mildly lined her big eyes with kohl. The girl beside her, with blonde bangs and light eyes, hides her smile. She shows the ticket in her hand to her friend, and says, "It stays here." She's not going to go forward and give it to the driver. A third girl says, "You know what? Basically, they keep women and men apart in buses so we sisters don't have to pay as much." The bus stops. An old man from an aisle seat on the driver's side gets off. The girl with a binder looks around, sits down, and puts her binder and books on her knees. The man sitting beside her is a young Afghan. He unblinkingly watches the crowded street. Now even the men's section is packed. I turn my head away. I see the bulky woman wrapped in the black chador sitting in the women's section. I stretch my hand towards the window to pull it down. I change my mind because the glass is too dirty, and I don't like to touch it. How many more stops until we reach the square? The bus halts. The woman with a baby in her arms gets off. A boy replaces her. We hear loud voices from the front section. The driver yells, "Move to the back! I can't drive like this!" The standing passengers reluctantly move back. The driver's eyes catch the girl with jet-black bangs. "Get up! You don't understand rules, you sit down whenever you want and they lay me off work for ten days ...," I try to make room for the girl with jet-black bangs. I named my son after the Joseph of the Genesis who had been thrown into a well. Is Yusef's well tighter than the mother dog's grave? I didn't hear a shot last night. I peep through the throng of women wearing headscarves to see outside. I press the button to stop the bus. The girls neither talk nor smile. When the bus halts, I struggle out and hop off.

At the corner of the square, I remember the time. A bunch of people are waiting for a taxi. They shuffle in one spot, or run after a taxi that is slowing down but is not going to stop, or ignore those standing ahead of them, or step back after realizing they're in the wrong place, or jostle in order to get on a taxi, or ... I pull the strap of my watch tightly pressing my wrist out of the sleeve up to the prescribed length. I'll be late and the machine will stamp red on my attendance card. Granny will be angry if she finds out I'm late for work. She thinks that if employees are late, their wages are not *halal* (lawful). When Yusef looks at her confused, she tries to keep her mouth shut. Then when her grandson's curiosity is piqued, she gravely explains, "Well, my dear, the whole mess in the world is caused by mixing what is lawful with what is unlawful." A passer-by treads on my foot. Granny loves to talk about such things, she just loves to talk. Shouldn't I tell her that my Yusef doesn't feel like talking anymore? But the turtle dove shouldn't remain silent when ...

A beat-up taxi stops in front of me. Several people get off. A male passenger remains in the back seat. I open the front door and sit beside the driver. I give him a side-glance. He's beardless, clean-shaven as men were under the Shah. "Straight ahead," I mutter. The taxi begins to move. The driver doesn't ask me, "Where to?" I give a sigh of relief. Maybe I'll reach my destination by the time the taxi gets too full. Is the passenger in the back seat fat or thin? It makes no difference. Men have the habit of sprawling. And if you happen to be in the middle, then ... But the worst happens when the man beside you tries to make the physical contact he's been forbidden to do, to vomit what he's been forced to keep down. The taxi stops. A heavy man with a briefcase gets on. The taxi starts. Approaching the intersection, the driver slams on the brakes. A pedestrian who's jumped into the street out of the blue keeps on its way, ignoring the driver's curses. My eyes catch the grinning face of the heavy passenger with the briefcase in the corner of the mirror. I look down. On the dashboard are stuck postcards with pictures of cats. I stare at them. After all, it's easier to watch cats than crows. The driver stops. Two male passengers run for the taxi. The driver turns to me. Looking down, he says, "Excuse me, madam, you should sit in the back." I don't move. Two passengers reach the taxi. "Just yesterday I got a ticket ..." the driver says, gentler than before. I open my purse, pay the fare, and get off.

I pass the empty reading room softly and slowly. The librarian at the circulation desk is napping to make up for the sleep he lost the previous night as a free-lance cab driver. I don't feel like greeting anybody. Looking down, I pass the stacks. When I open the office door, my workmate's holding the phone in her hand, making up for her lack of a phone at home. She half-rises. It would be a pity if she had to hang up. "A report of daily routines of the bridegroom to the mother-in-law!" says the circulation librarian when he isn't sleepy anymore and comes by the office. I pass my fingertip across the corner of the table to measure the dust. My co-worker smirks and shrugs her shoulders. I open the drawer. The paper tissue box is empty. I close the drawer and clean off my fingertip with the end of my headscarf. I examine the books piled up on the table. My workmate covers the phone's mouthpiece with her free hand and says gently, "You're back before the end of your leave!" I nod and smile — the mask of a repetitive morning smile. The cleaner comes to the room with a duster. She's still wearing black, though now wearing black is not a sign of mourning. I open the small window behind me and turn my chair towards the shaded lawn. The cleaner asks about my Yusef. What can I say about her Ismael? My workmate hangs up. After she says hello to me, she says to the cleaner, "You didn't come around yesterday. Everything's dusty!" "I went to his grave," the cleaner says hoarsely. My workmate picks up a book and leaves the office. Doubting my memory, I ask the cleaner, "Have they brought his body home?" The gnarled fingers are rubbing the duster hard against the table. "You know what kind of animal his father is. Even if they brought my Ismael home and he buried him, he wouldn't let me ...," she says. The tired hand stops moving. I point to the stool next to the shelves. She sits and leans her head against the edge of the shelf. I turn my head. Doesn't the sunshine ever fall on this side of the lawn? My workmate comes back to the office. I hear the creak of her chair. She turns on her transistor. She can't help listening to the "Home & Family" program. As she says, all she remembers well from all economic courses she took at university is Charles Fourier's ideas about the nature of satisfying jobs. A crow is wandering around the lawn. I turn my chair. The cleaner drags herself up and goes back to work. The radio host is interviewing a martyr's mother. My workmate turns up the volume, *Even if I had ten young sons, I would willingly send them all to the war ... for we're satisfied with what makes our saints satisfied ... and we're wishing for paradise...* The phone rings. The gnarled fingers knot. My workmate turns down the volume. I pick up a big book, *Stories of the Prophets,* and look through it. I find Abraham and his son in it. So Ismael is given to Abraham and is taken back from him and is given back to him. I close the book, which doesn't say anything about Hagar. My workmate hangs up the phone and goes to the stacks with a book in her hand. I turn my chair. The crow will never leave the lawn. "When was I ever a mother to my Ismael? After he was born, his father kicked me out ... over all these years I was separated from Ismael. I hoped that one day the draft would be over, and he'd come to me at last," the cleaner says. The tired hand drops. The gnarled fingers grasp the end of the manteau. "But yesterday?" I ask. She turns her head up. A vague smile appears at the corners of her lips, "I go to the graves of strangers. It makes no difference. Does it?" I get up. I pick up my handbag and head home.

### III

The cloud that made the day gloomy becomes rain at sunset. Isn't there any end to Jacob's grieving? Yusef's cracked lips move:

"Now the turtle dove will get wet for sure."

I close the window and say, "She'll find a shelter
... maybe. Can I pull the curtain?"

He nods restlessly. I let my hand drop. He asks:

"What was going on outside?"

"Nothing."

He looks at me in disbelief:

"Was that why you came back so soon?"

I put the jug of water beside him:

"I shouldn't have gone."

He raises his head from his pillow:

"But you said your leave was over."

I don't look at him:

"I won't go anywhere until you get well."

He asks, confused:

"Why?"

"... If you take your pill, it'll ease your pain and
you won't have fever anymore."

He puts the pill on his tongue. I give him a glass
of water. He swallows the pill and water and says:

"You're fed up with my sickness ... just like Dad
coming home late."

"But he comes home eventually and when he
does he brings you toys."

I sit on the edge of his bed. He says impatiently:

"But I don't want toys anymore."

I caress his unkempt hair:

"It's good if you sleep. I'm going to tell you the story of Joseph ..."

## IV

They kill the bitch, but the puppy survives. Does he survive? The new sound, the little sound. The eyelids wounded by light are closed in darkness. The shot shatters the darkness. They throw my Yusef into the well for the sin of being loved. So, who's going to interpret my waking and my dreams from now on? The shelves in the empty quiet reading room shiver like dogs and dusty books tremble. My workmate sneezes and dials a number. How many zeros does the phone number of the municipality have? In the moonlit night does the bitch leave the puppy alone and go to the vacant lot? Granny says that disaster always follows sin. Yusef looks at her in disbelief. The sword always hovers above the head. Nobody calls cats and crows to the trial. This is Joseph K., who should be punished. The taxi driver who doesn't stick pictures of crows on his dashboard should be punished too. But Raskolnikov looks for his own earthy punishment. Do I hear the sound of the front door? Is he coming home? Though Yusef doesn't want toys anymore. The cleaner pulls out the duster from her manteau pocket. Hagar gets lost in the dust of the old book. Granny says that not everybody's grave can be Ismael's grave. I wonder if Jacob is weeping for his own broken heart or for Joseph's coat. All the sky's clouds descend to darken the earth. Does the fire of fuel and a match's sulphur push back the darkness? Granny bites the stretched skin between thumb and index finger, wondering how Pahlavi shorts function as a veil! The girl who's used kohl as eyeliner shields her bangs with her binder. The fire that dies won't replace the sun. The evening rain wets the turtle dove. Granny says that eventually Joseph will be taken out of the well and Ismail will be given back to Abraham and … But the rain that makes earth and sky gloomy doesn't let Jacob have even a ray of sunshine.

They come and take the puppy away; the bitch remains. Does she remain? The hand stretched vainly in the air drops. The lost sound, the closed mouth. I move my head away from the sheet covering Yusef's legs. The bitch rejects her fate. Doesn't she?

# LADY WITHOUT LAPDOG

## I

Neither chador and burka in the style of the Qajar period, nor even a headscarf in the manner of Hezbollah, this thin cotton headscarf still bothers her, half its trail hanging straight down, half of it hanging loosely over the shoulder so it doesn't tighten up beneath the chin or stick to the scalp, an insignificant cloth rectangle folded in a triangle that controls and covers head and rebellious hair and sometimes when she goes to a court, her workplace, becomes an actual veil, fixed just so with pin, hair pin, and paper clip, pressing the top of her veiled body like a load of lead, sometimes forgotten in the daily routine, or in the fear and bewilderment of unpredictable events, this plain headheadscarf, which once was the mark of undesired but accepted respect in public demonstrations and then became an insulting humiliation in another demonstration, a flaming badge of Islamism to the foreign public and, to devotees of the regime, an undeniable proof of opposition to it, keeps hurting her.

Staring at her, Azita slowly, sweetly raises her porcelain white arms, thrusts her white fingers' red nails into the thick black hair around her face, slightly tosses the hair fallen to her shoulder, and gently says, "Poor darling!"

Blocking out the hubbub of the bright, spacious, busy transit hall of the airport, she bends forward to smoothe her skirt. Leaning back, she half-smiles at Azita sitting across from her in order to confuse her about what her smile means. She tells her, "This time I've brought only two manteaus with me. One is what I'm wearing, the other's for the conference."

Azita smirks about the maanteaus they have to wear. "Oh, really! You mean having lots of maanteaus is forbidden over there? But having lots of wives isn't forbidden?"

She raises an eyebrow. "Obviously you were once a family court judge! In the Shah's era..."

Azita interrupts. "Long ago we used to have things that we don't have anymore."

She tells her sweetly, "That's right. Now we have things that we didn't have then, though."

Azita nods. "Like this manteau and headscarf that function like a chastity belt."

She smiles. "That's why the slogan goes, 'The hijab is immunity.'"

"So now if you attended a medical conference instead of a law conference, you could give a lecture on how to fight Aids."

She replies instinctively. "Why me? Your brother's a doctor, he also attends medical conferences, he also ..."

Azita cuts her off. "And he's also my neighbour, true, but why should I lie? First, I rarely see this brother and neighbour. That's one of the disadvantages of the American life style, or maybe one of its advantages. Don't think that it's just the Islamic life style that has some advantages. Second, this brother and neighbour was once your husband apparently and before that your dear cousin. So you know perfectly well that he's not the type of animal to support anything or anyone, including himself. He's the type of animal who knows how to evade it."

She says bitterly, "I thought he only knew how to dodge a ball."

She gets up. Shaking her loose manteau, she takes a few steps to reach the window, and stares at the airfield, summoning faded memories. In the spacious brick-paved yard of the house in Amiriyeh neighbourhood, in the green plain of the cottage in

Ushan near Tehran, on the wet sandy beach of the villa in Babolsar on the Caspian Sea, or even in the long narrow lane of the Pamenar neighbourhoud, anywhere, they'd often team up to play dodgeball. Sometimes alone at night, in the midst of a disturbed dream, she still hears the clamour of those days and tries, behind closed eyelids, to catch a clear momentary image of the scenes. In the grey light of the sun, partly concealed in the distance, several shadows move. Azita and her brother Maziyar stand in front of each other and alternately aim the ball at her. She closes her eyes, crosses her arms, and tries to make a live image out of a pale illusion of a memory by blotting out her surroundings. Her memory still works well; more or less as well as it did during those gone years, when she could deposit unwieldy words from piles of bulky books, and take them out again as needed. Yet describing the past in her mind is like pouring cold water over it, not warmly imagining herself in it. She has trouble regaining this lost patch of her past -- a pure image, born of intuition not will power. A hand thrusts into a dark well and comes out empty. Not even her ears recall. She does remember well that Maziyar wiped his sweaty forehead with the back of his hand and said, "Bravo, you succeeded in getting hit!" Azita, always supportive, said, "If she wants she can play very well. She decided to get hit." Maziyar shrugged, impatiently stepped away, stopped, turned his head, and slowly said, "Dodge – means – dodge – ing!" And then, turning briskly on his heels, quickly said, "Understand?" This word, which Maziyar often used in arguments, was the final word too. When they played games that word had conveyed sympathy, but the last time they had argued it did not. Now she can't resurrect his voice or his face.

Azita pulls her sleeve and says, "We have lots of time before our flight, let's go to the coffee shop. It will make us look like distinguished people."

Following Azita, she mumbles, "Looking like me!"

Without turning, Azita says, "Lady, you look like your pockets -- loaded with rials. I wanna celebrate that you've been allowed to be an advisory judge by spending my pockets full of dollars."

She licks her dry lips. "When we get to be full judges, I'll invite you for a royal lunch at human rights' headquarters and spend all my rials."

Turning her head, Azita stares at her in astonishment. "What a thick skin you've developed!"

She sneers."Thick skinned and hard-headed."

Azita quickens her paces. "I didn't doubt that you stayed over there just because you were stubborn, but ..."

When they enter the cafeteria, she lingers and smells the scent of pastry, coffee, and cigarette. Looking around, Azita heads towards a table beside the dark glass between café and the transit hall. They hang their handbags on the chairs' arms and sit across from each other. Having ordered coffee and cake, Azita digs her cigarette case out of her purse and puts it on the table. In the mild light on Azita's face, she carefully looks at her and says, "You don't look younger than me, despite the fact that you didn't stay over there."

Azita wrinkles her forehead, keeps her head inclined, and leans her chin against her palm. "When two women meet each other after fifteen years, no doubt they exchange such compliments, especially when one is the other's sister-in-law."

Smilingly she says, "But I never looked on you as a sister-in-law."

"We were classmates and colleagues. Weren't we?"

She nods. "Always."

"What aaalways?" Azita's voice sounds sad.

The waitress puts down coffee and cake. After she leaves, Azita continues without looking at her. "I mean that then I thought you could tolerate the situation because you were so hard-headed. Other than the hejaab that bit our throats and all the other pins and needles they constantly poked us with, I couldn't stand seeing the mullah taking away my job the way they took my money and the rest of my life."

She sips her bitter coffee and teasingly says, "Well, if they can give you rights, they can take them away."

Azita turns and twists her fork into the soft cake. "It's hopeless. That they take your rights and then you get them back and then when you reach the end of the line you see that you're behind where you were when you started."

She puts a piece of cake in her mouth without interest and gulps her coffee. "Maybe it's better to jump out of the line rather than go backward. I don't know, I'm not sure anymore."

Azita finishes her coffee and slams the cup down on the saucer. "We loved our career. When they smashed our profession, you stuck around to take care of it, and I fled to the desert rather than watch it die."

She laughs loudly. "Since when did California become a desert?"

Azita lights a cigarette.

"Since Her Excellency, the former judge, with her assistant, His Excellency, the former colonel under the Shah, drudge from dawn to midnight running an

Eastern restaurant in Los Angeles, the navel of the West."

She looks intently at the lines on Azita's forehead and the wrinkles beneath the makeup on her eyes and gently says, "We're not in the same boat. We can sympathize with each other, though."

A wan smile appears for a moment on Azita's face. "Sure, both of us are losers."

In order to console her she says, "But you're not an absolute loser; you've kept your family."

Azita puffs her cigarette and sarcastically says through the smoke, "Definitely! That a feeble colonel still works hard to afford his son's tuition fee at Harvard, or that this stubborn boy is managable, should be appreciated. After fifteen years of eating Big Macs and drinking Cokes and smoking Marlboroughs and listening to Michael Jackson, if you still keep your family, it means you did a good job. However... "

As good as a professional story teller, Azita pauses, puffs her cigarette leisurely, and stares at her in silence. Gradually the trace of sadness leaves Azita's face.

She asks curiously, "What goes after the 'however'?"

Azita clears her throat and makes a face. "Well, I should admit to Your Excellency that although we exiles don't cover our entire bodies, we cover our spirit."

She twines the black headscarf's trail in her fingers and disagrees. "But in this part of the world, what's common is disclosure, whereas in that part everything's concealed."

Azita smiles and interrupts her. "Oh, yeah. These Westerners are constantly talking about their scandals in their lives and we in-betweeners have to learn not to hide the dirty stuff."

She whispers, "So, you're alone too!"

Azita shrugs. "Basically everybody is alone. What bothers me is that now I have empty hands."

Confused, she says, "But you're free to do whatever you want."

Azita puts out her cigarette. "You don't deny personal inhibitions, do you?"

"Of course not, but we have to face our own too."

Softly smiling, Azita says, "Well, it's easier to fight the enemy you know."

"You always know how to evade this kind of question."

Azita gestures for the waitress and says, "I chose once and thought ahead. When you chose Maziyar you did it unthinkingly. By the time you realize the implications, you'll have grey strands around your temples. But I figured out what was going to happen."

She asks impatiently, "What do you mean?"

Azita stares at her. "I always tell you what I haven't told myself yet."

She pushes away the cup and the plate and quickly says, "Tell me now in case we never meet again."

Azita hesitates. "Or I may think like that in order not to have any regrets."

She frees her handbag from the chair. "Like what?"

Azita clears her throat. "I said to myself: 'Be honest, lady! What you lack is a romantic love, not a physical fuck. As long as this lover doesn't fall from the sky, don't sin!"

She smiles. "What a shame your Persian has gone to waste in exile!"

Azita puts her cigarette case in her purse. "True, it's wasted. But I haven't converted it into the Tehrangeles dialect."

In order to comfort her, she says, "You still have time."

Azita takes out her wallet. "Oh, yeah! Up to the last moment, I have time but who knows! Maybe the Angel of Death will be my Prince Charming."

Suddenly, swallowing tears, she feels a lump in her throat. She says nostalgically, "How could I have done without you for so long?"

Azita looks away from her eyes full of tears. "Shit happens, but time hasn't passed us by. What will we two modern teenage girls do if two experienced gentlemen happen to come to our way?"

She smiles bitterly. "We'll run away."

Azita half bends and says, "So don't look back. Let's go!

## II

She cannot sleep. Azita's words have made her restless. She's pushed back her chair, but she cannot lean against it as comfortably as Azita did and fall asleep as easily as she. She feels uncomfortable because her ears are blocked, the maanteau and headscarf make her hot in the stale air of the plane, the yellow light is harsh, and the taste of cold food lingers in her mouth. She gets up. She shakes her manteau's skirt. She stretches to relieve the pain in her back and shoulders. She looks around. She doesn't spot the small group of men with unshaved face, closed collars, and Samsonite briefcases. When she'd seen them in the transit hall, she pointed them out to Azita and said, "You see, not only we women but men like them have their own kind of uniform!" Azita grudgingly looked at them and replied, "They're not singled out like us, though." When she lined up to board the plane, carefully looking at passengers, she spotted only this group as regime officials. Among the Iranian passengers, all the women, other than two or three old women who kept their patterned scarves in the style of pre-Islamic era by knotting them under their chin, make themselves look like Westerners before boarding the plane of a foreign airline. She'd said to Azita that she wanted to err on the side of caution by wearing the headscarf despite the fact that she didn't like to be conspicuous and it was unlikely that she was being watched by those men, at least on her way to the conference. Azita had protested, "But you're not going to the conference as their representative!" She'd nodded, "No, I'm not. But I'm planning to come back, and not sit in a corner of my house. I can't do anything with a cancelled lawyer's license!"Azita had angrily replied, "That certificate isn't so important. Watch that they don't cancel your birth certificate!" She'd smiled. "Many things have changed." Azita had asked, "Principles too?"

She looks at Azita's familiar face. She doesn't see any difference from the way she was before, other than now the pale lines are deep lines. She turns her head away. She goes to the washroom and washes her face. She's too tired to fall asleep. She can read as long as lights are on. When she leaves the washoom, she encounters one of the men with unshaved faces. The man clears his throat and looks down. Involuntarily, she pulls her headscarf forward. She rushes back to her chair. Azita's chest moves up and down to the rhythm of her gentle breathing. The young black-haired couple sitting in the row behind them, hand in hand, leaning against each other, are asleep. She doesn't see rings on their fingers. The happiness and peace on their faces prove they are sure of each other. Before taking the seat, she gazes at Azita again. Azita's bitter expression isn't new.

Azita, carefree, strolls ahead of her. She grabs the sleeve of Azita's school uniform, yanks it toward herself, and says, "Hey, Azi, hold on. I want to tell you something!" Azita's books and notebooks fall and scatter on the ground. They kneel on the curb to collect them. Azita mumbles, "Why did you do that?" She whispers, "I just wanted to show you that guy." Azita asks loudly, "What guy?" She blushes, "Why are you so talking loudly? I mean that guy from the Dramatic Arts faculty; he's standing over there at the entrance." Now Azita has her books and notebooks organized in her arms. "Well, he's there every day." Countering Azita's indifference, she says, "He's sure not waiting for you." Azita regains her good mood and links arms. "No, he's waiting for Vidaa the Dummy." She says argumentatively, "Other than you, Aazam the Bear, and me, all the other girls in our class have some sort of boyfriend." Azita laughs, "You're so stupid! They're just crowing like roosters." She makes a face for Azita. "So, you're saying that all of them are liars?" Azita imitates her Granny's voice and says, "Believe me, girl, it's good to have wisdom. They tell lies either to you, who are naïve, or to themselves, who are just as naïve as you." She says indignantly, "You just say that to keep yourself happy." Azita isn't in a bad mood at all. "As Granny says, 'God knows you're not like me, somehow you have a boyfriend." She pales. "Why do you fib about people?" Azita laughs. "Not about people, about my brother." She says angrily, "If he thinks that I'll wait for him seven years until he comes back, he's mistaken! By the way, who says that I'm in love with him?" Azita nods seriously, "I didn't say that."

She feels a shooting pain in her temples. She gestures for the flight attendant. When the attendant comes by, she asks for a glass of water. She opens her purse to get a pain killer. She happens to see Azita's old book. She decides not to take a pill. She picks up the book, carefully touching its yellowing pages. The margin of the cover's left corner is burnt and there are several big and small stains around the big bold words of *Selected Stories of Anton Chekhov*. She turns the page and reads the table of contents. She's read all of them at least once or twice, but long ago. Maybe when the book had just moved from the bookstore to Azita's bookcase. Good stories read long ago are like precious souvenirs in an old lady's chest of drawers; they are perfect, but if you take them out of their niche, their charm disappears.

Azita takes off the borrowed manteau, throws it on the bed, sits on the edge of the couch, opens her handbag, and takes out the book. "Don't you think that my Granny have the honourary title, 'Mother Antiquity'? For thirty years she's kept my room just as it was. She's done the same with Maziyar's room. Like Mrs. Havisham in *Great Expectations*, she roams around her worn-out dusty furniture." She asks, "What book is that?" Azita hands it to her. "I went there to weed out some of my old museum stuff in Granny's when she was away, but I couldn't throw this one out. I read it again. You should, too!" Suspicious, she asks, "Why? You mean it's especially significant for me?" Azita laughs. "Oh, no. *'I just remembered those days we had ...'* It's good to have a change. Since you write too much about crime and murder and law and non-law, you've ended up looking like subsection *n* of clause *s – s* standing for 'shit'." She puts a cup of tea on the table. "But you read whatever I write." Admitting it, Azita waves her hand, "From start to end. After reading the first piece I said, 'Colonel, what's happening over there?' After reading the second one I said, 'Colonel, what's wrong with this girl?, After reading the third one, I banged my fist on the table, and said I should go there and find out what's so wrong with her that she's confronting them." She asks, "So, after all these years, you've taken a long trip to see what's wrong with me." Azita sets down her empty cup and lights a cigarette. "Sure, first I wanted to poke my nose into what's happening here but, second, in my exilic corner, I missed you and my Granny very much." She says angrily, "Please don't talk about exile and nostalgia like other people! After all, you still claim that you're concerned about justice and fairness. To choose between here and there has been to choose between exile and more exile for everyone, in a way to choose between bad and worse. So don't complain any more. There are so many colonies all over the world, so many different kinds, even where one is born and gets accustomed to its ups and downs. That you complain about misery attacking us is one thing and that you constantly feel sorry for yourself is something else. If somebody prefers to leave rather than stay, for whatever reason and reasonably or unreasonably, it doesn't make sense to complain about it!" Azita stands and applauds, "Well done! Your defense is wonderful; however, it's rushed and irrelevant. But since hunger has now overcome this particular former judge, let's wrap it up and make peace.

Both of us are exiled and both of us better not nag; it's much much better if we adjourn. Now, tell me, are you going to feed me or not?"

She drinks the water that the flight attendant has given her and puts the glass in the chair pocket. Azita hasn't moved. The lights go out. Without reading the book, she puts it back in the bag.

After putting the dishes in the sink, she says, "You can't find a better host than me. I'm so sleepy and tired I may faint." Azita protests. "No way, I've come to your place so I can chat with you til morning; I can't chat with my poor Granny anymore." She apologetically says, "Sorry. Believe me, it's been a long day!" Azita shrugs. "None of my business! If I get dead tired at midnight after a whole day of unpleasant work, that makes sense. But it doesn't make sense for you because you sacrificed everything and everybody for your delightful work..." She interrupts, "If by 'everybody' you mean your dear brother, I have to say that he wasn't good for me." Azita lowers her voice. "I know. But he once loved you; you thought so yourself!" She says gently, "*He* thought he loved me." Azita nods. "He thought he loved you; he loved you in his own way. To tell the truth, when I was living here, I thought that generally in the struggle between wife and husband the woman's in the weak position, because tradition and religion and law all backed up men senselessly; yet, over there, it's vice versa. So I've gradually become a supporter of oppressed American males." She dries her wet hands. Coming out of the kitchen, she says, "You mean Maziyar has become Americanized." Azita shakes her head. "Not at all, he's the same phenomenon he was before. But because I wasn't here there's something in your relationship that hasn't become resolved." She sprawls on the easy chair and says in a bored tone, "I'm ready for the interrogation." Azita clears her throat. "Oh, I'm your legal-aid counsel. Ironically you didn't obey your husband in the land of Islam by choosing where to live and thus, according to *sharia*, you were a disobedient wife, which amuses me a lot. However, my question is that if the husband obeyed you and yielded to what you set up, then don't you think that your scale of justice would tip down?" She yawns and says, "You think so because you think too much about the miseries of American males. Other than in our childhood, there was always a sort of distance between Maziyar and me so we didn't see each other well. Basically both of us were following our own dreams; the issue of staying or leaving became an excuse to break up. You know perfectly well that I don't understand either obedience or dominance." Azita asks desperately, "So you're sure?" She firmly nods. "Be sure that at least after fifteen years he doesn't have any doubts either. Now let me put an uncensored pure American movie in the VCR for you so that I don't feel sorry about going to bed." She gets up. Azita lies on the couch, "It's not an action movie, is it?" She smiles, "Oh, no! It's the American version of the Iranian movie, '*Mr. Halu.*' Azita asks, "Is it *Forest Gump*?" Astonished, she asks, "Have you seen that?" Azita raises an eyebrow. "No, I haven't. You told me about it yourself."

She closes her eyes. Memory still pushes back sleep.

Next morning at breakfast she asks Azita, "How was it?" Azita's mouth is full; she looks at her but doesn't reply. Before they go out for the day, Azita, wearing her borrowed manteau and headscarf, stands pointed towards Mecca and, imitating her Grandma, pounds her chest. "O, Lord, would you have been less divine had you offered my maritally unsuccessful cousin and me a crazy-romantic Romeo exactly like this American actor?"

## III

The next seat has stayed empty. Now that Azita isn't with her, she can sit in the window seat and look at the deep blue of the ocean as long as there's light. She doesn't remember any moment over the past two weeks that she thought of Azita at all. She was so focused and anxious because of her work that she didn't have time for anything else. She's just found her own way to do things in her job. She shouldn't give up. When Azita left, she'd said, "Azi, don't expect to hear from me until I get back to Tehran!" Azita had raised an eyebrow. "So you mean you're not changing your mind and stopping on the way to stay with us." She'd hugged Azita again so that they wouldn't see each other's wet eyes. Then Azita had turned her head away and whispered, "Well, it's better to be a crazy workaholic than to be crazy about some Juliet." She swallows the lump in her throat. No, dull blue doesn't appeal to her. She wants to watch beyond the plane's window the Mediterranean blue, or just to slide her eyes over the silken hills of clouds. So, should she give up this desire like her other desires? Although she's worked hard over the past two weeks, she knows that her weariness and confusion aren't due to it. When the flight attendant brings drinks, she changes her place and sits by the aisle. The friendly smile of the elderly Belgian, sitting in the aisle seat of the middle row, encourages her. Cautiously glancing ahead, she doesn't spot the blond, middle-aged guy who'd given her a disgusted look when he passed her in the transit lounge and spat on the shiny floor. She knows

that his seat is a few rows ahead. The seats of her Dutch
colleague and of Gurov are also rows farther ahead.
When Gurov approached her half an hour ago to chat
with her briefly after the flight started, she could have
told him about her fear. However, at most, and even if
he thought her fears were not groundless, he would only
have said something to encourge her. After all, there
were limits to a Westerner's manly protection. The
friendly elderly Belgian would be a more reliable refuge
in case of need. The Belgian had directed his eyes to her
black headscarf and nodded in sympathy. She'd
involuntarily yanked down her headscarf and tucked
her loose strands of hair out of sight and lectured him
about personal liberties, hoping to stifle her anger with
his approving nod. What she hadn't told the old man
was that her lecture at the conference was too radical to
let her dare violate the dress code rule now, and this
compromise was an Eastern tactic. The old man,
politely listening, had patted her shoulder in a fatherly
way and said that racism, the residue of human
ignorance, could be found anywhere. She had calmed
down and said that encountering an enemy was just a
small matter of bad luck.

To have met Gurov as well, even if it was a sign
of good luck, was trivial. After the trip, again swamped
with daily duties and routines, despite the fact that you

once got a hello, a word, a look, a smile, and the address of a friendly stranger, you now were unwilling to drop him a line or find any excuse to do it. Nevertheless ... She feels suddenly warm. She shakes the trail of her headscarf in the air restlessly and lets her head and neck feel the air. When Gurov, leaning over the back of the empty seat ahead, was looking down at her with a smile ... Oh, no, definitely no, she mustn't fall for him. She leans her head back against her seat. Won't it become a well, so long as the void remains covered? She closes her eyes.

Azita, just arrived, asks her, "What the hell have you been doing, staying single all these years!" She smiles, "Lots of people envy it." Azita looks at the framed picture on the mantelpiece. "Probably one of them is me. This woman, our innocent chaste grandmother, frowning in the lens of a *non-mahram* photographer, certainly wasn't upset because she was alone. Was she?" She turns toward the picture. Azita continues, "She was a lady without a male guardian for fifty years!" Defending her late grandmother, she says, "God bless her soul, our poor grandmother sacrificed getting a man in order to remain a lady. Many women become ladies without paying the price, and some women are ladies merely due to their men." Azita rearranges the pictures. "Since both of us are optimistic good-natured grandchildren, we don't doubt that our grandmother deprived herself of some things over so many years. But, since I'm nosy, I ask you, 'What about yourself?'" She looks at Azita in confusion. "What do you mean?" Azita, without turning, says, "That woman kept one eye on herself in order not to sin, and the other eye on Heaven. 'What about you?' means 'What do you do?'" As always, Azita's frankness surprises her but she doesn't react. Azita makes a face, smirks, and says, "You have the right to remain silent." She laughs, "I answer my lawyer's question." Azita turns her head, "So?" She pulls apart the linen curtain and says gently, "I swallow."

She opens her eyes. Gurov, half bending, smiling, has said that he'll be back: he could sit on the empty seat beside her, and they could talk about the movie they saw last night, *Dark Eyes*, with Marcello Mastroianni. She doesn't see anybody in front of her. She turns her head listlessly. The well-dressed Belgian is napping. It's night. She hears the gentle laughter and whisper of the couple sitting next to the old man and looks at them. They are kissing and cooing. She notes in surprise the lines and wrinkles of their faces. She turns away head and closes her eyes.

Azita raises her eyebrows and widens her eyes. "I'm not talking about a perfect Prince Charming, but you mean not even a half-perfect Prince Charming has fallen into your net?" She shrugs her shoulder, "I haven't been hunting for one, nor is one findable." On a night when they stayed awake until dawn because Azita'd kept her awake, she told her the story. "Yes, on my last trip, I think I saw a Prince who was the twin of Gregory Peck, or maybe he was just himself. It was an evening I stayed at a hotel, and then, hearing someone whistling a familiar tune, I went to the window. He was leisurely walking his dog and looking up. When he saw me he lingered. He nodded and smiled at me and then went on his way, still whistling." Azita, lying on her stomach on the couch, holding her chin in her palm, asks, "What was his dog like? Was or wasn't he better than his master?" She nods, "The dog was very cute, but as soon as I yielded to temptation and looked out the window at 5 p.m., it squatted ..." Azita laughs. "So, Prince Charming's dog was indiscreet." She says in irritation. "It took a crap. As soon as I was admiring it, it defecated. That apallled me. Although it was too hot at night, I had to close the window lest the smell of its poop kept me awake. I tried to think only about Prince Charming."

She senses that somebody is standing beside her. Embarrassed, she opens her eyes. The flight attendant has brought her a pillow. Disappointed, she doesn't return the flight attendant's smile. Before putting the pillow behind her head, she involuntarily looks at the passengers sitting in the middle row. The old man is still sleeping and the old Romeo and Juliet are still on the job. Once again she closes her eyes.

Sitting with legs crossed in front of the TV, Azita angrily turns it off. "Both sides are wrong." She replies, "Well, the extremes are two sides of the same coin." Azita slides her fingertip over the flowers in the rug's design. "If you pay attention to American movies and commercials, you'll find all the sex disgusting, no matter how well it's blended in." She puts an apple from the slopes of Shemiran on the plate next to Azita's hand. To find Azita's favourite apples she'd looked all over the Tajrish bazaar in Shemiran and when, she didn't find it, she went to the Behjat-Abad bazaar and found it there. She says, "When you sit in front of this magic box, you're not supposed to use your brain. No matter what part of the world you are in." Azita picks up her apple and smells it enthusiastically. "The brain of a nosy animal like me works automatically. For instance, when I see that these infidel Westerners pamper their dogs so much and highlight 'screwing' – as my Granny used to say – so much, I conclude that sex equals dog. Overseas it's overvalued so much that not only does it show off its cuteness but also its shit. Whereas here it's a taboo, invisible during the day, but you can hear it howling at night from any corner and hole and closet and attic."

She feels sleepy. Maybe the Dutchman is still awake. Gurov said that the Dutchman was an old friend of his. Later yesterday, after he'd invited her to see a movie, she asked, "Is our Dutch friend coming with us?" Gurov said, "He was supposed to come, but he fell asleep." She hesitated. "Isn't it too late?" Half smiling, Gurov said, "Come on, I bet you'd like it." The first day of the conference, she'd arrived late because she was tired; she'd slept late. She'd been shown the room where her committee met. The committee chair was the same heavy grey-haired American woman with whom she'd had several talks on her previous trip; she knew other two committee members, one of them from India, and the other from Holland. Gurov was the only new committee member, and although the American lady introduced him as Finnish, at the break she'd asked him, "Haven't you come from Russia?" Gurov hasn't been friendly, but after a while she's noticed that he's the only one in the group with whom she can talk about anything other than professional topics. And ... now if he comes and sees her with her closed eyes ...Does it mean that she shouldn't fall asleep? She remembers the folk tale of "The Old Woman and Uncle Nowruz", how in the spring, the New Year, an old woman waits for an old man, Uncle Nowruz, to come to her house and bring the new year. The old woman cleans up the house and prepares everything for her beloved guest. She knows that she shouldn't fall asleep. Otherwise, he'll pass her by on his way to others' homes. The old woman doesn't want to miss seeing him, but she falls asleep and ... Without opening her eyes, she involuntarily shrugs. Maybe it's Gurov who has fallen asleep. Gurov had said, "You must have taken me for Russian because of my name." She nodded but hadn't said anything. At night in the quiet unfamiliar hotel room, she'd turned over Azita's old book and reread the story of Anna and Gurov. Even if Chekhov had wanted to tell the story of a distressed Anna, the story has become Gurov's. On the evening of the last day of conference, she said to Gurov, "I thought you might be Russian, for you have the same name as a character of Chekhov's." Gurov hadn't reacted with more than a side glance and a half-smile and then had said that they'd see each other at the airport tomorrow morning. No, the story hasn't been the story of Anna and how she found her lost half; it's Gurov who feels a revolutionary change. But if the Russian Gurov can make a fire from a spark, this Finnish Gurov seems to be only a firefighter. Nevertheless at night he comes to her unexpectedly. She says hesitantly, "But tomorrow morning we have our flight, both of us." Gurov's stare has pushed back her remaining doubt. She's said, "I'll be ready in a minute."

After watching the movie, Gurov accompanied her to her room. She hasn't replied to Gurov's gentle "Good night." She's just closed the door softly behind him, gone to the window to look at the moonlit night, and, filled with the atmosphere of the movie, chewed her index finger's nail angrily.

If the Dutchman had fallen asleep, or Gurov hadn't fallen asleep, they could have talked about the movie, or, as Gurov called it, "The Story of Marcello, the Italian, about the adventures of Gurov, the Russian". Definitely she should tell Gurov that she thinks the difference between the story and the movie doesn't just arise from the difference between an Italian lover and a Russian one. The difference also comes from the difference between that time and this one. Bonds are looser now and no sin, even Marcello's, is major. It is Anna's film, Anna with her bad life and luck and with a lapdog that is not the symbol of luck, but a symbol of a lost dream. When Gurov had said before the movie theatre became dark that one couldn't see *Dark Eyes* without having a lady with dark eyes for company, she said smilingly, "But this lady doesn't have a lapdog." When did the taste of Gurov's nice words become bitter to her? When she'd looked at the ring on his finger in order to avoid the stare of his light eyes? Or, when she'd sunk her face into the pillow to swallow her tears because of not having a lapdog? No, even if the Dutchman had fallen asleep, or Gurov hadn't fallen asleep, she couldn't have talked about the lapdog and how she regrets not having one. But if Azita had been there ... Or, if somebody from the dark narrow path in front of her had come softly and intimately to her ... Her tired hand listlessly makes a semi-arch in the stale air and heavily falls to the emptiness beside her. The shadow of the lapdog fades behind her closed eyes. The lady without lapdog sinks into darkness.

# WHERE IS SHEMR?

I hear footsteps from the corner of the lane. Where is Shemr, who struck down Emaam Hoseyn, the Third Emaam, the hero of Shi'a, at the Battle of Karbala, and then cut off his head? Where is Mokhtar, who revolted against Shemr and Emaam Hoseyn's other enemies? I have to go to the yard and pick up a pebble from the flowerbed and wedge it in the front door to keep it open. Then I can sit on the wide low bench with peace of mind. Mother has done a huge pile of dirty laundry from morning till noon, so she is now dead tired. She doesn't hear the drag of my slippers on the brick-paved yard. The summer afternoon is wonderful. My mouth has become dry. I wish the ice seller would come and give me a handful of ice. To crunch the ice between my teeth is marvellous. Feeling like a nap because of heat and their full bellies, the men have gone to lie down under the ceiling fan. Grandma, taking along her straw fan, her prayer book, and a bowl of water with a lump of ice in it, has gone to the basement. After only reading a few lines, she covers her head with her white flower-patterned *chaador-namaaz* and starts snoring. Now I bet she's sound asleep. After washing the dishes, Mother has left the *paashir,* the basin under the tap in the basement kitchen, to go to take a nap. Then the house is mine alone. I prefer the lane, though. I didn't notice who had come and gone.

The lane is quiet. Zeynab's kids, who usually hang out in the lane from morning to evening, haven't shown up. I don't feel like playing *yek ghol dow ghol,* the pebble game, by myself. I also don't have charcoal to draw squares for hopscotch. Today I don't feel like playing anything. Where is Zeynab, who was named after the heroine of Shi'a, Emaam Hoseyn's sister? It's been a while since Zeynab started to go to Esmaa'il Bazzaaz St. or King Square. She says she sells more lottery tickets in busy places like those. Wednesday fast approaches. Good for someone whose lucky day is Wednesday! May he give his luck to me! No, to Zeynab! Zeynab says she has bad luck. Fatol, her brother, used to say, "My sister's hand will bring good luck. Anybody who buys a ticket from her will win, if not big money, at least five tomans. Our house only has a small pool. "We don't have enough water to make it worth it to hire Fatol to drain it," says Father. But if Fatol doesn't come to this neighbourhood, who's going to empty rich Haaji Qomi's big pool? Where is Fatol?

The cement top of the wide low bench beside the door is too hot to sit on. Snaking below the narrow blue slot of the ceiling in the lane, it's like a colourless, shapeless fire among the yellow pot-holed path, the sunburnt brick walls of houses, the dirty water of the channel in its midst. It burns the skin as if I've fallen into a bakery oven. The heat wave strikes my body from all directions. They've recently made curbs for the channel. A *musaa ku taghi*, a turtle dove, just flew down from the house across from me and perched on the channel's edge. It looks like it's walking on the pebbled floor of the oven; it rapidly hops and shakes its head.

The turtle dove reminds me of Musaa, the kabab maker. "Musaa is hard on Zeynab. How can he justify himself on Doomsday?" Mother says. Zeynab sometimes curses him. Most of the time she curses her own bad luck rather than Musaa. I thought that Musaa, the kabab maker, was like the brutal Shemr. But I couldn't believe it. "Musaa hasn't sinned. If he's the oppressor, who's the oppressed?" says Grandma. But I know how soft-hearted he is. The other day when I went to the little bazaar to buy bread I saw him sitting in a corner of his store and applying some antiseptic to the wounded wing of a dove. The way he looked at the tiny dove in his big hand made me embarrassed that I'd thought badly of him. I assumed his eyes were full of tears; his eyes are small and round and black and shine like buttons. But Shemr cannot be soft-hearted, nor Yazid, the caliph who defeated Emaam Hoseyn.

Grandma says that across all eternity there was not and won't be a person crueler than Shemr. She says although it's right that love of worldly pleasures made Muawiya's son Yazid blindly destroy the Emaam, it was shameless Shemr who caused the calamity to the Prophet's family. It was accursed Shemr who began atrocities, misery, and blasphemy against the servants of God. Yet Grandpa used to say that divine wisdom ordained that a nasty inferior guy like Shemr appeared and martyred the King of the Religion so that all the sins of Shi'a Muslims might be washed away.

So, what about Shemr's sin? So, who's guilty, if Shemr isn't? Moreover, Musaa the kabab-maker is not Shemr. What happened to Fatol isn't his fault. But isn't it Musaa who oppresses Zeynab? Isn't it he who has taken Zeynab's kids away from her? Zeynab's kids look like the kids of Moslem, Hoseyn's follower and cousin, killed in the Battle of Karbala. Musaa's house looks like a prison in Shaam, old Syria. Musaa the kabab-maker is bad. He is cruel to Zeynab. That is to say that he's become unkind to Zeynab since Aa Taghi died and Zeynab wouldn't agree to marry Musaa, his brother. He said that if Zeynab didn't accept his offer, he wouldn't give custody of his brother's children to her. Musaa the kabab-maker is ugly and has a badly shaped body. His thighs look like bolsters. When he walks, his stomach shakes like a water skin. His double chin's flaccid and greasy. His skull is bald and red in the middle. His body smells of meat and onions and the fat from sheeps' tails. Poor Zeynab! "I bet Zeynab will never yield to an unfair ruling!" says Mother. "But so what? If she's really concerned about her children she shouldn't be so stubborn to reject the offer. Who can be a better father for her children than her brother-in-law? That she's constantly weeping and cursing will bring no good!" says Grandma.

What was the verse recited on the Night of Strangers, in mourning for the death of Emaam Hoseyn? Something like this:

*It's tonight that Zeynab, the daughter of The Best of Women*

*Weeps and mourns more than other nights.*

But the day before yesterday, Taasu'aa, the Ninth of Moharram, the eve of Emaam
Hoseyn's martyrdom, Zeynab didn't weep. We went together to watch *dasteh,* the procession of mourners for Emaam Hoseyn. Mother was sick. Zeynab was down-hearted. She didn't cry. "What colour is today?" I asked her. "What?" she said. "What colour is today's kite? Everyday has a different kite, you know," I said.

She didn't reply. The kite the day before yesterday was not light or dark grey or dusky like the kites of hot weather. The kites of summertime are big and light; they look like sunshine lighting the world or the full moon. Their tips and tails are long like the plaits of Gord aafarid in the Shaahnaameh epic. Their tips are up at the end of the sky, their tails on the earth. Some of the rings of their chain may be darker, yet when you look at them you cheer up, for the rings are colourful: yellow, golden, orange, pink, red or blue, bluish-green and turquoise. The kite on the day before yesterday wasn't like them. It wasn't thin and transparent like tissue paper. Nor was it colourful. It was deep orange-red, beautiful, but not light. It was restless. Its ears twisted. Its nose was slanted. It headed towards the earth, but then changed direction and went up. It was uneasy. It waved its long narrow tail and lashed against the sky. Maybe it was afraid of The Night of Strangers. Zeynab didn't cry. She was uneasy.

At night in the little bazaar of Naayebolsaltaneh the air was filled with the smell of sweaty bodies and rose water. At the end of d<u>asteh</u> the procession bore the weighty metal *alaamats* covered by a shawl and hand-woven *termeh*. Atop them were <u>*laalehs*</u> the crystal tulip-shaped candleholders and metal birds. Each bird had a feather in its crown. I wanted to count the feathers. I failed. Boys, wearing black shirts and headbands and carrying candles in their hands, walked behind the alaamats._The tiny colourful flames of candles were twisting and twirling. They became wide and narrow, long and short. Like a school of fish in orange, dark blue, golden, and silver, they gently moved ahead in the midst of a big black sea. Chest-pounding lamenters, wailing mourners, chain-flailing flagellants slowly followed those tiny colourful fish like horrible huge whales. Lantern-carriers and torch-bears walked in the final row of the dasteh. The lights of lanterns and torches looked like roses. The hands of lantern- and torch-bearers looked like a wind current. The heavy slap of hands, the clatter of chains, the clash of cymbals, the hoarse moans of the wailers, and the intermittent sobs of women linked and spread the sorrow of the family of Seyyedolshohadaa, Emaam Hoseyn, the Lord of martyrs, as if it were rose water. Beside the street's lamppost, the old woman, bent and covered by her flowered white chaador-namaaz, loudly wept. But Zeynab didn't cry. Grandma, unable to stand for long, sprawled on the ground beside me, was pouring out big tears and sniffling rapidly to prevent her nose from running. I gnashed my teeth so hard that the edge of the chaador tore between my teeth. Zeynab's eyes weren't moist. I wished I could burst into tears. I had no tears, though. It's always like this. I try hard to bring tears, at least one teardrop, to my eyes during the mourning months of Moharram and Safar or in the mourning ceremony held in the fourth day of the month at Haaji Qomi's house but I fail. At the latter, Grandma constantly and rapidly sheds tears while she constantly and rapidly cleans the small glasses and saucers with a little bit of boiling water and serves tea. On the protruding brass belly of the samovar Grandma's face becomes distorted and funny-looking. The tap of the samovar drips and the drops of boiling water fall into the brass bowl. I suppose Zeynab and I are the only ones who don't shed tears. I wonder whether why Zeynab doesn't shed tears is because she is too busy to listen to the sermon, or like me because she cannot weep. The female servant at Haaji Qomi's house doesn't do anything on mourning days. She says that it isn't a good omen for her if she works then. I don't know why during the sermon I pay all my attention to either Zeynab, who prepares the hookah for women, or the preacher who relates the disasters of the Battle of Karbala. When I listen to him but don't look at him, his mourning gives me the impression that he is sitting thirstily in a tent of Emaam Hoseyn's family, deeply depressed because of the atrocities that Shemr and Ibn S'ad's, Yazid's general, committed against him or, as if amid Karbala's catastrophe, he's beside the wounded teenaged Ali Akbar, Hoseyn's son, calling on the Emaam with him, or he's gone with Hazrat Abbas, Hoseyn's brother, to fetch water. When the story reaches the point when Abolfazl's hand is severed, one imagines that his hand is severed. When Harmaleh in Yazid's army struck the neck of Ali Asghar, Hoseyn's baby son, one imagines that he hits his own baby. When he describes the bazaar of Shaam or the Yazid's court, one imagines he's gone there in a caravan of captives. When he talks about the breast of Omm Leylaa of Hosyen's family, full of sorrow, and the heart of the newly married Qaasem, Hosyen's nephew and the Prophet's grandson, devoid of joy and the burning sighs of little Roqiyeh, another little girl of Hoseyn's family, the women's wails reach the sky. Leylaa, the cook, scratches her cheeks. I assume she recalls her own son, who died when he was young. The whites of her bulging squinting eyes take on the colour of blood. Leylaa's son was a teenager; he was not Ali Akbar. He wasn't a martyr; he died of tuberculosis. Leylaa was lonely after his death. "I've lost the light of my eyes, not because of the smoke of the oven, but because of this loss," she says. I wonder why I feel depressed when I see Grandma's eyes full of tears, or Leylaa's cheeks covered with scratches, or Zeynab's frown and pursed lips. As long as the preacher speaks and women recall their own grief, I

don't think about Karbala. But when the sermon ends
and the women have no more tears to shed, I feel blue.
Zeynab doesn't weep, though.

Now there is shade on the corner of the wide
low bench, but the sunshine is still hot. On 'Ashuraa,
the Tenth of Moharram, I went to watch *t'aziyeh*, the
passion play commemorating the martyrdom of
Hoseyn, with Grandma and Leylaa the cook. The
*tekyeh*, built for its performance, was packed. People
swarmed and jostled. The chaador
had fallen from my head over my shoulders. I was
sweaty. I couldn't breathe. I was kicked and jostled that
much that I felt flustered. I'd held Grandma's hand
covered by her chaador. Hustling, she went on. She
ignored curses and swear-words. In the midst of the
hubbub came the sound of drums and reeds and
cymbals. I trod on the foot of a plump woman with a
pockmarked face. She hit my chest with her elbow. A
moan rolled up in my larynx. With one hand, I was
dragged toward the path Grandma cleared; with the
other, Leylaa pulled me. The sun was so hot that I felt as
if a big burning charcoal was sizzling on my head.
Finally Grandma and Leylaa the cook stood up, Leylaa
on tiptoe. Her protruding eyes rolled in a way that
scared me. Looking at her, I was afraid lest her eyeballs
would jump out and tumble like two big marbles. It

seemed to me that Leylaa and Grandma had found a gap among the packed crowd to peep through. Leylaa's hand that had held my wrist hard relaxed. Suddenly she yelled with her piercing voice, "Oh, Abolfazl, I wish I could sacrifice myself for your severed hand!" Several women, standing in our front row, turned back and gave her a dirty look. One of them said, "Shut up, you ugly hag!" Leylaa the cook didn't care. As if she hadn't heard it. Motionless, she stared fixedly. Grandma's dry cracked lips were budging, but no sound emerged. I felt like crying. I couldn't see anything but the cotton chaador of the pockmarked woman. Her chaador was mouth-eaten. The small flowers of her purple chaador had five petals. The tip of my nose would have touched her fleshy back if I hadn't pulled my head away. A small young woman, standing beside me and staring ahead, said, "Now it's time for the person who reads Shemr." I could see that she had dark skin and an ink-coloured mole at the corner of her lips. "Who's the person who reads Shemr?" I asked. Grandma didn't hear me. I pulled her chaador hard; it slipped down her head. Her henna-coloured hair shone red under the sunlight. She was embarrassed and quickly pulled the chaador over her face. She looked at me angrily and said, "What the hell are you doing, you bad girl?" "Because I don't see anything. Tell me who the person who reads Shemr is,"

I said. "Sweetie, he's the one who looks like Shemr.
Move a bit this way so you can see something through
the crowd. Or you can stick to me so I can tell you what
I see," she said. "I want to see the person who looks like
Shemr. What does he look like?" I said. The dark-
skinned woman hit me in the side and said, "Shhhh!"
Grandma frowned and told her off: "Gosh! In this
racket, is it only this little kid who has to keep quiet?"
Somebody said, "Sister, say salavaat, humble respects to
the Prophet and his Family." Grandma pulled me a bit
further. "Now, Abolfazl has come to the centre of the
field. May God blind both eyes of the one who's going
to cut your hand off!" "Why on earth are you cursing
him? It isn't real. Is it?" I said. It seemed to me that she
didn't hear me. She started to sob. The women's
shoulders shook from their weeping. While sobbing,
Grandma kept telling me intermittently what she saw.
She kept telling me, then she'd stop and become silent,
suddenly shocked, as if she forgot what she was
supposed to do. I was restless because of heat and the
smells. While she told of Ali Asghar, the nursing baby, I
smelt sour milk. I was nauseous. Told about the young
Ali Akbar, I smelled something strange. As if I saw that
the blood oozed through a small hole in front of me. Or
maybe it was the red shirt of Shemr. Suddenly Leylaa
withdrew her hand from her chaador and put it on her

breast. With her complexion as yellow as turmeric and her face as wrinkled as a crumpled sheet of greasy paper, she folded on the ground. When the person who recites "The Oppressed" came on the scene, my heart began to beat hard. What is Emaam Hoseyn supposed to look like? His shawl and his turban are green; his cloak is white and spotted with blood. I anxiously thrust my nails into my palms. I was biting my lips hard. I felt a lump in my throat. I couldn't swallow my saliva. I closed my eyes, hoping to see the Emaam's face in mind; I failed. All I could see were gently shifting dark and light spots. My ears were full of wailing as Shemr rushed towards Hoseyn's tent. His voice sounded like the thunder. It made everybody shiver. Everybody was dead silent. I could see through the gap some legs rapidly going back and forth. "Where is Shemr?" I said. I tried to speak but couldn't. My burning palms had become moist. As if Grandma's black chaador had become a flame. When the Zeynab's throaty voice sounded, Leylaa the cook suddenly stood up. The pupils of her eyes shone. Her skin had become as white as plaster; her thin lips full red. Pulling her chaador, I asked, "What does Zeynab look like?" "She's covered with black, from top to bottom. You can only see her eyes," she replied. But Leylaa sounded as if she'd seen Zeynab's face very well!

Who the hell is the one who looks like Zeynab? Who does Zeynab look like? Why can't I find counterparts for Zeynab and Emaam and Shemr? The other day Grandma and Haaji Qomi's wife and I went to the Aaghaa's house to ask a religious question. On our way back I asked about it, because Grandma had said, "Haaji Qomi's wife is a believer and very pious. She knows the answers to all religious questions. Good for her! I wish I was like her! She'll have angels for company." I thought she surely knew the answer. When I asked, she readily answered, "Well, it's clear, honey. May God let me be sacrificed for the Emaam, he doesn't have any equal. He is a saint. What a pity that now there is only the Twelfth Emaam." "But what does he look like?" I insisted.

I can't imagine him unless I learn who he looks like. Good for those who see the Emaam in their dreams. I tried to see him in my dreams, but I failed. "If you want, you can wake up before dawn and sweep the threshold of the house and keep doing this for forty days so that the hidden prophet Khezr will appear and make your wish come true," Grandma said. No way! Aside from the fact that it's not easy to wake up before dawn, the problem is that I know well that Khezr won't appear if I sweep. One should be a believer. Well, I wanted to be a believer, but while Grandma was passionately telling about what to do and what not to do, Mother burst into laughter. She distracted me. She looked as if she was teasing three of us — Grandma and Khezr and I. Grandma got annoyed. Mother stopped laughing. I lost my belief. Now it's useless. "If you have even a bit of doubt, it'll be useless. Your faith will disappear like smoke in the air. Faith is not a ring that you lose today and find tomorrow or buy another one to replace it. It comes to you all of a sudden and leaves you all of a sudden as well," Grandma says.

Haaji Qomi's wife swallowed. She shook her head. She gathered the hem of her expensive chaador so it wouldn't get dusty. "He is ... oh, what can I say. Surely, he's tall. Wide shoulders. A narrow waist. His arms ... his arms ... his arms ..." she said. Her voice had deepened. Her big hazel eyes had widened. She moistened her lips with the tip of her tongue several times and started stammering. I stopped to listen to her. I was distracted by the purple clusters of acacias hanging over the wall of her house. The particles of light, smoothly and gently spinning ahead of me disappeared. My faith had been lost!

The old cotton beater appeared at the corner of the lane. I turned my face to the wall and closed my eyes. I was on the alert to hear when his footsteps would end. He didn't have enough energy to yell. Instead of calling loudly, "Hey, cotton-beating..." he moaned as if he carried the heavy bow and mace of the mighty hero Rostam on his shoulders. My eyes closed, I easily imagined him. He has a swollen gland beside his ear that looks like a ruby-coloured potato. He always keeps a basting thread attached to the gland. Also, he sticks the needle in the edge of the collar of his dirty canvas shirt. His worn-out percale pants have patches on the knees. The soles of his cotton shoes have holes. The old cotton beater looks alive when he beats cotton; he grins. His toothless gums are red. He moves about like a magpie amid beaten cotton twisting in the air like snowflakes. He swells his sunken cheeks and sings along to the movement of his hands and body. His voice, vibrating and ringing, like the sound of his bow, spins in the air. The yard becomes full of dandelions. Yet, when he starts sewing, he becomes silent and as lethargic as when he wanders around the lanes. Again, he looks old and ugly and scary. His thin long legs stretch so much that you think that he is a hobgoblin who will jump on your shoulder and wrap his legs around your neck. I feel frightened, but his footsteps die all of a sudden — like my faith. I turn my face towards the quiet lane.

"Do you know what a hobgoblin is?" I asked. Fatol the pool cleaner was pulling out buckets of muddy water to empty it into the channel in the lane. "You mean you know?" he said. "It's like the old cotton beater," I said. He put the bucket on the stair and, confused, stared at me. He looked upset, or frightened, or depressed. He pulled his shoulders forward, hunched his back, picked up the bucket and moved on. I ran after him. "Well, if you know, tell me how he looks like," I said. He stopped again. He wiped his sweaty forehead with the back of his hand. With a low voice, as if he didn't want to be heard, he said, "I guess it's like this damned disease that I have, cause it doesn't leave you alone until it breaks you down." He looked at me in a way that bothered and depressed me.

The neighbours, old or young, tease Fatol. After it was rumoured that Fatol would frequently turn up at Haaji Qomi's house because of his daughter, Zahraa, they redoubled their teasing. The other day, when Fatol was sitting in the vestibule of Haaji's house to rest, some kids kept making fun of him until he had an epileptic fit again. His convulsed face scared children and kept them away. His body had become as stiff as wood, and his arms and legs shook. Foam poured out of his mouth. Then he fell on the ground unconscious. Nobody noticed how Zeynab had appeared. The children ran away as soon as they saw her. We wondered how she had showed up at that time of the day. Maybe she had a sixth sense.

Zeynab comes to this lane every evening before going to the *yakhchaali,* the area where there used to be icehouses, then were used by poor people as shelters. She finds an excuse to stop by this or that neighbour and chat with women in the hope of seeing her kids. Musaa has asked his mother to take the kids in and not to let them be in the lane when Zeynab appears. Zeynab doesn't give up. She will peep into windows if she doesn't see them in the lane. If this doesn't work, she'll go to one of the neighbours and ask her to convince Musaa's mother to take the kids to the lane for a while. "This girl hasn't had a good moment in her life from the start. She was an orphan. Before marriage she had to work hard in this or that house to raise poor sick Fatol. Then she married = Taghi to escape poverty. But he ran out of luck, he became bankrupt. Then he died of sorrow and left Zeynab alone with two kids. Now she has the burden of this half-witted Fatol on one hand and the cruelty of that monster on the other," Mother says.

"Why did they name you Zeynab?" I asked. She moved her worn-out cotton chaador a little over her head and sighed. Her lips looked dark blue. She had dark circles under her eyes. She bit the corner of her lips and said, "How do I know? Maybe my Mom knew that I wouldn't have anything other than disaster in my life." When she said that, I felt sudden excitement. My ears became hot. I said to myself, "What will I see if I close my eyes?"

The day of Taasu'aa, the ninth of Moharram, Zeynab was upset. That evening she didn't cry at all. At noon on 'Aashuraa she was alone. During the afternoon of Aashuraa, before the four-o'-clock-flowers would open, Zeynab came and said that the severed head of Emaam Hoseyn was going to be displayed at the tekyeh in the Paamenaar neighbourhood. Grandma had gone to the Shah Abdolazim Shrine. Mother was sick. Zeynab and I went to Tekyeh. It was packed with seated people. The front rows were full. We found a seat at the last row beside the curtain that separated women from men. As soon as somebody shook the curtain or pulled it up, there was a fuss. The curtain was black. Zeynab was grumpy. She didn't move her lips. She was staring at a point in front of her. I was on the alert to jump up and stand on tiptoe at the right time. Everybody said something. The thin voice of the man reading the Koran got lost in the rustle of the loudspeaker and the fuss of women. Men weren't silent either. They murmured. My legs had got numb. I didn't dare move because there wasn't any room. Women sweated a lot. They talked loudly. They fanned themselves with straw fans and watched their shoes in case they could be stolen. Several boys in black distributed water among the crowd. The margin of the sky was still reddish. Zeynab was too grumpy to be asked anything. I was excited and restless. I was all ears. An old woman with a puffy face and narrow eyes said that the severed head of the Emaam had been displayed at this very tekyeh last year. When it got dark, they lit glass lanterns. Everybody got bored because of waiting so much. Nobody listened to the Koran. For no reason we turned our heads. Zeynab didn't move at all, though. She stared ahead as if she was sitting in a movie theatre. All of a sudden the lights went off. Many jumped up, including me. Somebody from back pulled back my chaador. Then a quarrel started. At the very front, where the head of the Emaam was supposed to be displayed, a green pale light came and went. It appeared and disappeared again. Zeynab had been standing up too. My chaador fell over my head. I was standing on tiptoe. My eyes were wide open. Suddenly I felt a pain in my right ankle. My knees bent and I fell over the old woman with the puffy face who was sitting in the front row. She screamed and everybody turned their heads towards us. She smacked my head with her palms. I was too shocked to feel pain. I wondered how Zeynab pulled me out of her grasp.

The moonlight had turned the walls blue when we got to the lane. "Did you see that?" I said. Zeynab stopped and stared at me. As if she was deaf and dumb.

Then she turned and narrowed her eyes and looked at the entrance of Haaji Qomi's house. The lane's electric light was broken. But a big round yellow lamp at the doorway of Haaji's house was on. I saw mosquitoes around the lamp. Suddenly Zeynab screamed and ran towards Haaji's house. The lane was quiet. I panicked. I ran after Zeynab. In the corner of the vestibule Fatol was crumpled. His head had bent over one shoulder. His bucket had spilled beside him. I was so frightened that I couldn't breathe. As if dead, Fatol didn't move. There was foam around his mouth. A line of blood ran from his temple towards his neck. Each of his shoes had been hurled into a corner. Zeynab knelt at his head. She didn't cry. I ran for home. My tongue was dry and stuck to the roof of my mouth. My body had become cold. The hair on my hands was standing up. The door was open. I went into the corridor. The white petunias of the flowerbed in the yard looked blue under moonlight. Grandma appeared at the threshold of the room. "You're back, sweetie. You saw Seyyedolshohadaa? You saw the persecuted Emaam?" Her voice was nostalgic. The air smelled of petunias. Grandma's eyes were shining, they looked wet. My lips couldn't move. I leant my back against the wall and sat. I nodded. Where was Shemr? Where was Mokhtaar?

## *ALL THE DAYS OF GOD*

At dawn Dorbibi, of the town of Zaabol, Baluchistan, heads toward town. Having barely been able to get a seat on the worn-out minibus, she sneezes — the narrow lane is dusty, and there's a pile of dirt in front of the newly built mosque. The sneeze is a sign of impending bad interruption. She is obsessed with the temptation to turn back; she doesn't have the energy to move, though. As if today is different from other days. Last night she didn't sleep well and tossed and turned. This morning, she got up weary and bad-tempered, put the kettle on the brazier close to Nazar Ali's bed, washed her hands and face, put on her chaador, and went out.

No, there's no rush to get to work. Everybody knows that she's not punctual. Besides, she's perfectly aware that she's not greedy. That she keeps going to a few houses to work as a cleaning lady is mostly out of habit. She isn't even in a rush to go to the Na'lbandaan Bazaar and eat grilled liver. Although last night she hasn't eaten anything other than a piece of bread and a bowl of yogurt, she feels stuffed. Today, she doesn't even feel like chatting. On a dirt road full of potholes, she's staring absent-mindedly at the landscape beyond the stained dusty window of the bus.

Having reached the main road, the driver's helper twists one of his long sideburns and says, "Dorbibi, you're not O.K., you look lousy!" He then bursts out laughing. He's absolutely wrong if he thinks that he can provoke Dorbibi into replying roughly, or to start complaining or talking. Zobeydeh, the beggar, laughs as well. Dorbibi doesn't turn her head. She knows that, as always, Zobeydeh is sprawling at the back of minibus and has seated her kids around herself. Zobeydeh doesn't pay the fare, so she's not allowed to sit. She is so insistent that Qaasem, the driver, has given up and let her have a ride. Zobeydeh has brashly taken over Haaji Khaan's sheep-cote. Zobeydeh is not from Alang, this village. Although in her youth she migrated here to find a job as a cotton picker, she's never stuck to a job. And now if someone keeps asking her, she straightforwardly says that producing puppies is one of a beggar's professional skills. No, Dorbibi hates to see Zobeydeh – not because she is a beggar or sleeps with this guy or that guy. Zobeydeh's lousy life isn't enviable. But Dorbibi doesn't know why it upsets her to see Zobeydeh's two chubby sons, who always have runny noses. She involuntarily casts her eyes towards the sons of Mash Taqi, who go to town every day to find jobs as construction workers and always nap on the way. They're sitting behind the driver. Having watched their broad shoulders and the thick suntanned back of their necks, she bites her lips.

Well, surely, it's her fate to be so lonely and have no support. Whatever it is, she's been accustomed to come and go and eat and sleep by herself and be on her own; she doesn't feel like feeling sorry for herself at all. It isn't clear to her why she feels down today. She feels her head is too heavy for her body. Her stomach is upset. She feels sharp pain in her temples, her legs are numb, and she's short of breath.

The edge of the road slips by quickly. Trees and shrubs and cotton fields all fast recede. The seat beside her is empty. The driver's radio is on. Chickens in a basket for the market, which the squint-eyed Asdollaah will sell, don't stop clucking. She feels delirious. She leans her head against the back of the seat ahead of her. Her chaador slips down her scarf and rests on her shoulder. The felt hat of Dad Bemaan Ali who's sitting in a front-row seat, smells damp. The newly visible sun is weak. The dark green of soybean leaves makes her nostalgic. To recall old time isn't helpful. The wind and desert and sharp sunshine and cloudless sky and pale shadows — shadows of her mother, whom she lost too soon, the shadow of her father who disappeared, the shadow of her brother who ran away to the mountains, and ... the shadow of Nazar Ali, the young lad with a dark complexion and a scar who appeared out of the blue and caused her to migrate. A cloud gradually comes and covers the sun's face. If the wind blows and brings the smell of grass and freshness, maybe she'll cheer up.

The bazaar is busy and noisy. Since she arrived, Dorbibi has been hanging around villagers who are selling and townsfolk who are buying. She doesn't feel like going to the lady doctor's house. Dorbibi first thought that maybe she didn't feel well because she was starving, so she went to Moraad and ate two skewers of grilled liver with a piece of bread the size of a hand and a bowl of *dugh,* watered yogurt, then when she felt bad and her stomach went sour and her head got dizzy, she went to the stand of Ayaaz the cotton-beater and listened to him babbling for half an hour. She feels nausea because of the bazaar's many smells. Her legs have become as heavy as bolsters and lack the energy to move. She is surprised how lethargic she feels. Over a lifetime she's suffered because of Nazar Ali's disability and her daughter Maahbibi's illness while she's been proud of her own good health and energy. Dizzy, feeling bad, she walks among the crowd. No, today, she doesn't have enough energy to do the laundry and clean windows; despite the fact that the lady doctor would fill her purse and stuff her bag with used clothes for Maahbibi's kids. Why the hell should she pay Maahbibi's medical expenses? Let her husband do it for once.

She goes to the side of the road and waits for a ride. The weather is cool, and the sky is overcast. It's drizzling. She belches. She waves for a bus. The bus hurtles by. The bus's horn annoys her. She curses. She rubs her knees with her palms. She hears a noise in her ears. Her eyes see black. A van stops at her feet. The son of Rahim, the cattleman, peeps out of the window and smiles at her. A wan smile appears on her lips. She grabs the bars at the back of the van and pulls herself up with difficulty. She sprawls in a corner among sheep's dung. She prays she won't faint before she reaches Alang. The cool cozy corner of her room with a rug and brazier and kettle and tea pot could have been a perfect paradise if she hadn't a husband with infected eyes and cracked lips and paralyzed legs.

She feels a heavy sudden pain in her chest. She clenches her teeth. She mustn't panic. Now it's showering. She holds her palms under the shower. There is no reason to worry. This rain would fill her empty hands exactly as it does now, even if Nazar Ali hadn't gone to steal field cantaloupes and hadn't returned with a back that a spade had hit, or if poor Maahbibi had got healthy. She had been wrong to feel that today was different from other days. Even if paradise were somewhere else and not in Alang, she would feel well as soon as she gets home and for this, she should be thankful. That's right, if she survives the last two or three kilometres, she will feel fine again. No, she mustn't be pessimistic, for all the days of God are the same — even if Dorbibi gets as old as this walnut tree at the side of the road that now passes her eyes so quickly.

# APPOINTMENT AT HOME

"The power went out again," said the man, and became quiet. The little girl who'd just gone to bed cried, "Where are you, Dad?" and whispered, "It must have happened." A cat's shadow loomed outside the window, and the green marbles of its eyes glowed and passed along the sill. Then all was dark again, but a geranium pot toppled and shattered. The man leaped to his feet. He wanted to say, "Don't panic!" but he couldn't.

"I'm coming," he murmured, dragging his feet. He blindly looked for the flashlight and found it after a while.

"The darkness scares me. Light a candle, Daddy!" said the girl.

"I'll bring a flashlight."

"Please light a candle, Daddy!"

Reluctantly he got the candle and matches. He lit a candle and said, "Now, you can rest easy! Move your pillow so your head's away from the window!'

The girl sat up. She moved her pillow and smiled. "Towards Mecca?"

Her grandmother had always insisted in sleeping pointed toward Mecca. She used to say that the Angel of Death might arrive any moment, no matter if it was day or night, or if you were awake or asleep. The girl used to place her pillow by the window. She wanted her grandmother to do the same so that not only could she hear her story but hear her breathe. But her grandmother refused to do that. The girl asked her first, then started to plead with her, and ended up arguing. Finally, she made up her mind not to speak to her. Her grandmother chuckled and said, "What a stubborn girl!" Annoyed, the girl replied, "Like you." In the dull light of the dark red bed lamp grandmother nodded and sighed, "I'm waiting, sweetheart. I don't want to be surprised. Nobody knows when he arrives and when it's time." She asked, "Who are you talking about?" Her grandmother answered, "I'm talking about death, honey, the Angel of Death. Would you like to hear a story about how he turned up in Samarra?"

Now she put the pillow away from the window and beat it with her small fists like her grandmother. Then she lay down. "You sleep beside me tonight. Don't you, Dad?"

The man nodded. The yellow and orange of the candlelight thickened against his pale face. His lips were tight. His anxiety mounted. The window pane was empty of moon, stars, and clouds.

The girl, like her grandmother, lay on her back, pointed towards Mecca. She pulled the blanket up on her chest and stared at the man. "Why don't you smoke, Daddy?"

She didn't hear a response. "Are you scared, Dad?"

"Go to sleep, sweetheart! Would you like to hear a story?" the man said, trying to make his voice gentle.

"What story?"

"The story of the fairy king's daughter."

"You don't know that one."

"Of course I do. If you keep quiet and listen, I'll remember it."

The girl turned her head away. A night without moonlight, a long wall, a small candle, a long shadow. She felt her skin crawl. She turned over and asked, "It comes from Baghdad. Doesn't it?"

"Maybe it doesn't come."

"Yes, it comes. It comes from Baghdad."

The man thought, "It comes from the sky," and said loudly, "Close your eyes!"

"Don't you turn on the radio?"

"Why?"

"Well, there might be a siren..."

"Nowadays they come without a warning."

"Could you see me through the window when you were on the plane?"

"Nope!"

"Could you see our house?"

"Nope!"

"What did you see?"

"Black dots, or coloured ones. Small or big."

"Those dots, were they people?"

"The people were dots. When you're up in the sky, you're a giant and people are dots. Or you're Gulliver and people are..."

The little girl excitedly interrupted him, "But, Dad, Gulliver didn't trample on Lilliputians, or crush their houses..."

"Gulliver lives in stories and movies."

The girl was aware of that. She felt cold all of a sudden. Her voice was broken. "That's why I don't like stories any more. In stories..."

Her voice ceased. Boom! It was as if the black balloon exploded in her body, her head, or her heart. It exploded and the shock waves spread. She crumpled in fear beneath the blanket.

The man harshly said, "Close your eyes!"

"Dad, I don't want to die with my eyes closed."

The man turned away. "We're alive," he said, his voice quivering.

The girl felt cold again. She trembled. She bit her lip and said, "Daddy, I'll close my eyes and sleep. I'm grown up. I don't panic."

The man, waiting for the second boom, didn't hear her. Another black balloon exploded and sent shock waves. The third balloon, the fourth one, and then a deep silence... The man slowly extended his hand and caressed the girl's soft tousled hair. "Now it's time to go to sleep! The game's over."

The girl, eyes closed, didn't move. The man moved away from her bed. He lit a cigarette. "The game's over." It was not a lie, not completely. He leaned his head against the wall. He closed his eyes. "The Angel of Death!" A moan escaped from between his clenched teeth.

The girl felt cold again. She said to herself, "This is not the Angel of Death." Her grandmother used to say, "Never believe I'm afraid, sweetheart. No, I'm not afraid of the Angel of God."

The man felt he was being crushed by a dense cloud of gas. His cracked lips moved. "It comes from the sky."

The girl, unmoving, said to herself, "It comes from the earth."

The man felt as if his chest were being torn open, and his heart was an open grave into which vultures spat morsels of the dead. He moaned again. "The Angel of Death!"

The girl couldn't stand it anymore. She opened her eyes. "He's not the Angel of Death, Daddy."

The man didn't hear her. The girl helplessly said to herself, "Maybe he's Satan." Her grandmother had always said, "At first Adam was an angel, and Satan was an angel too. Then Adam was Satan, and Satan was Adam..."

She moved a bit and said loudly, "Why don't you sleep, Daddy? Are you still waiting? He doesn't come again tonight. Does he?"

The man opened his eyes. He nodded. He barely raised his cold hand to touch the girl's cheek. "Why don't you sleep?" he said softly.

The girl held her father's cold fingers and said gently, "I sleep only when you sleep."

"You're not scared. Are you?"

"No, I'm not."

"You're not afraid of anything. Are you?"

The girl paused and then dared to say, "I'm afraid of your fear, Daddy."

"How do you know I'm scared?"

"You could sleep if you weren't scared. Am I right?"

"I'm not sleepy," he whispered apologetically. The girl's eyes looked sleepy. "OK. I'll lie down and close my eyes. Look! Is that OK? Now both of us go to sleep soon. OK?"

The girl put her arm around her father's neck, "Uh-huh," she said sleeepily.

The man didn't close his eyes. He tried to breathe quietly. He stayed motionless until his daughter's sleep seemed deep. Then he gently moved her arm away from his shoulder and withdrew.

The girl moved. "Are you sleeping, Dad?" she asked without opening her eyes.

"I'm sleeping."

His voice sounded weird to himself. "I guess this is the night of the dead and they're all coming out," he said to himself.

The windowpane was black. The candle had gone out.

The power hadn't come back yet.

The man wanted to get up and go to his own bed. He couldn't. He lay on his back, pointed toward Mecca. He closed his eyes. He put his palms on his chest and pressed down.

The girl moved in sleep. "Are you here?" she murmured.

The silence was not broken by a voice. Somebody rose to his feet at the entrance to the room and nodded that he was there.

# Afterword:

## The Refusal to Forget: Stories, Cities, Silences

Mahdi Ganjavi

Fereshteh Molavi is one of the most accomplished and uncompromising literary figures of her generation in contemporary Persian literature. A novelist, short story writer, translator, essayist, and bibliographer, she has made lasting contributions not only to Persian-language fiction but also to the intellectual and cultural life of the Iranian diaspora. With the addition of three new stories, this edition of *Stories from Tehran* offers renewed entry into a body of work as formally rigorous as it is emotionally and politically resonant.

For nearly two decades, Molavi has steadfastly refused to subject her writing to state censorship. This principled defiance led her to found Azadan Publishing in Toronto—an independent press committed to literary freedom. Azadan is more than a publishing platform; it is an act of resistance, a space of unmediated expression where works are published without compromise. Through this endeavor, and through her sustained literary activity, Molavi has charted a path defined by integrity, defiance, and aesthetic clarity.

Her most recent Persian novel, *Kamin Bud* (*In the Beginning Was the Ambush*), exemplifies her artistic ambition and political sensibility. Chronicling the formation and dissolution of a family across key historical moments—from the pre-revolutionary 1970s to the aftermath of the Green Movement—the novel weaves multiple voices and temporalities to reveal layers of memory, power, and fracture. Written over five years and described by the author as her "last arrow," it is a haunting work in which the border between reader and character, past and present, vanishes. Its language is refined and unflinching—a testament to Molavi's rare ability to disappear as author so her characters might emerge with piercing clarity.

Molavi's fiction is grounded in the belief that literature is not a decorative supplement to life, but one of its core mediums—a space where we think, remember, and resist. Her work often turns to the domestic sphere, not as a site of retreat but of psychological and political tension. Her characters navigate routines shaped by the sediment of gendered labor, historical memory, and emotional residue. The textures of the everyday—dishwater, cheap detergent, synthetic fabrics, soft fruit—acquire symbolic charge.

The external world presses against the body until the line between inner and outer life begins to dissolve.

Her narratives rarely pivot on dramatic incident. Instead, they unfold through the slow pressure of time and the intrusion of memory. A gesture, a scent, a sound—a minor detail might trigger a cascade of recollection or grief. Past and present do not follow chronology, but are layered through repetition, association, and fracture. Her stories mirror consciousness: recursive, uncertain, attentive, and alive with contradiction.

What makes her fiction so affecting is its tonal mastery. Her narrators do not confess—they endure. They observe, withdraw, and sometimes revolt. Her prose is spare and emotionally restrained, allowing feeling to accumulate through suggestion rather than declaration. Emotion emerges in silence, in tension, in the space behind a door or the sting of an unseen memory. Each story is finely calibrated: intimate, unadorned, and quietly devastating.

Molavi writes from a tradition that takes literature seriously—both in form and in ethical responsibility. She is acutely conscious of language: its elasticity, its history, its distortions. She resists simplification. She refuses commodification. Even her most subtle pieces are formally bold—marked by shifting perspectives, temporal disruptions, dreamlike ellipses, and moments of slippage between waking and sleep, memory and hallucination. Her fiction does not merely recount what happens—it examines how perception bends around what has happened, and how the weight of experience shapes what remains possible.

From her base in Toronto, Molavi remains a vital force in diasporic literary culture. Her public presence— especially her ongoing conversations via Clubhouse— reflects a lifetime of community building and intellectual generosity. She mentors emerging writers, fosters dialogue, and insists on literary and moral seriousness in an age when both are increasingly devalued.

*Stories from Tehran* stands among Fereshteh Molavi's most essential works. With the addition of these new stories—*Where is Shemr?*, *All the Days of God*, and *Appointment at Home*—the collection grows in emotional intensity and thematic reach. Each piece draws from a distinct geography and sensibility: the first, a child's search for justice and meaning in the mythic residues of Karbala and contemporary cruelty; the second, a slow-burning meditation on female endurance, bodily collapse, and the quiet dignity of a woman's laboring life in Baluchistan; and the third, a chamber piece of war-haunted intimacy, where a father and daughter cling to stories and each other amid the threat of annihilation. Together, these stories deepen Molavi's exploration of memory, care, violence, and the aching desire to remain human amid history's erasures. They remind us that literature, like mourning, is an act of fidelity to what refuses to be silenced.

The stories in this volume represent a selection of Molavi's fiction written up to 1998, prior to her immigration and the beginning of her exilic life in Canada. Since then, she has continued to contribute significantly to Persian fiction and has also written in English—for instance, her contribution to *Bantalogy* (Comma Press, 2018), and most notably, her novel *Thirty Shadow Birds* (Inanna Publications, 2019). These later works extend and complicate her diasporic vision, engaging themes of migration, gender, minoritized gender identities, and the shifting contours of language and home. Read together, Molavi's body of work traces a powerful arc of literary resistance and remembrance—one that crosses borders, languages, and silences to illuminate what endures.

Mahdi Ganjavi
Toronto, 2025

# ABOUT THE AUTHOR

Born in Tehran in 1953, Fereshteh Molavi lived and worked there until 1998 when she immigrated to Canada. She worked and taught at Yale University, University of Toronto, York University, and Seneca College. A fellow at Massey College and a writer-in-residence at George Brown College, Molavi has published many works of fiction and non-fiction in Persian in Iran and Europe. She has been the recipient of awards for novel and translation. Her first book in English, *Stories from Tehran*, was released in 2018; and her most recent novel, *Thirty Shadow Birds,* was published by Inanna Publications in 2019. She lives in Toronto.

# Asemana Books

*Devoted to Publishing Diasporic, Underrepresented and Progressive Literature on the Middle East.*

Email: Asemanabooks@gmail.com

Webpage: asemanabooks.ca

---

## Scholarly and Academic Research

- *Tanglusha of a Thousand Images: Essays on Culture and Literature* – Reza Farokhfal – 2024

- *Language, People, and Society: Iranian Minority Languages and Literary Traditions* – Edited by Amir Kalan, Mahdi Ganjavi, Anisa Jafari, Lale Javanshir – 2024

- *Music on the Borderland: Remembering and Chronicling the 1979 Revolution's Shadow on Iranian Music* – Keyan Emami – 2024

- *Implications of Class Analysis in Capitalist Imperialism* – Mohammad Hajinia and Shahrzad Mojab – 2024

- *Dark Night and Phoenixes of the Ashes: Nima Yushij's Poetry from 1932–1942* – Ramin Ahmadi – 2024

- *Whispers of Oasis: Likoo's Poetic Mirage* – Mahdi Ganjavi, Amin Fatemi, Mansour Alimoradi – 2024

- *Hafez and Irony* – Reza Farokhfal – 2024

- *Kurdish Women at the Core of the Historical Contradictions on Feminism and Nationalism* – Shahrzad Mojab – 2023

- *The Peasant Uprising of Mukriyan 1952–1953: Consulate Documents, Diplomatic Correspondence, and the Press Coverage* – Amir Hassanpour – 2022

## Critical Edition

- *The History of Changes in Iran* – Mirza Agha Khan Kermani, edited by M. Rezaei Tazik – 2024
- *Rostam in the Twenty-Second Century* – Abdulhussain San'atizadeh Kermani, edited by Mahdi Ganjavi and M. Mansouri – 2017

## Poetry

- *Shape of Extinction* – Poetry of Bijan Jalali, Translated by Adeeba Shahid Talukder and Aria Fani - 2025
- *One Hundred Nights of Yearning* – Mansour Noorbakhsh – 2025
- *Songs of Barbad* – Amir Hakimi – 2024
- *With My Shadows, I Created Myself* – Hadi Ebrahimi Roudbaraki - 2024
- *Citizens of September* – Saeid Rezadoust - 2024
- *Wonder of Memory* – Amir Hakimi – 2023
- *Galaxy Has No Memory of the Sunset* – Mahdi Ganjavi – 2023
- *Strangers Who Live in Me* – Mahdi Ganjavi – 2021
- *Exiled to the Rocky* – Ali Fatolahi – 2018

## Fiction & Plays

- *Escape from the Girl's Complex* _ Mahbobe Mousavi – 2025
- *Yousef, Joseph, Guiseppe* – Ali Foumani - 2025
- *An Iranian Odyssey* – Rana Soleimani – 2025
- *Lead to Evil* – Javad Alavi – 2025
- *We Are Drunk and Broken, and No One Is Witnessing Us* – Mahdi Ganjavi – 2025
- *Someone Had Died in Front of Our House* – Akbar Falahzadeh – 2024
- *Zinat* – Vahid Zarrabi Nasab – 2024
- *Siberian Crane* – Ali Foumani - 2024
- *Elephants Reached the Plain* – Kaveh Oveisi - 2024
- *Textual Mosaic* – Marzieh Sotoudeh – 2024
- *Expectations of a Dream* – Mahdi Ganjavi – 2020

Asemana Books is devoted to publishing diasporic,
underrepresented, and progressive literature on the Middle East.

asemanabooks.ca

www.ingramcontent.com/pod-product-compliance
Lightning Source LLC
Chambersburg PA
CBHW030540030726
47495CB00004B/1070